# SEE THE UNSEEN!

# GHOSTS OF ROCKVILLE

## Search for the Dominion Glass

### By Justin Heimberg

Published by Seven Footer Kids
247 West 30th Street, 2nd Floor
New York, NY 10001

First Printing, June 2011
10 9 8 7 6 5 4 3 2

MagicView™ is a trademark of
SevenFooter, LLC
Manufactured under license from
Digigraphics Technology Inc.

Cover Illustration by Greg Call
Design by Junko Miyakoshi

ISBN 978-1-934734-48-3

**GhostsofRockville.com • MagicViewBooks.com**

*For Dad*

# What People Are Saying About
# GHOSTS OF ROCKVILLE

"A feast for the intellect and imagination…"

—Dr. Christopher DeSena, *Detroit Gazette*

"Educational and uplifting…"

—Lawrence Zbysko, *Omaha Times*

"A…remarkable piece of…literature…"

—Paul Katz, author

"Brilliant and staggering! An astonishing masterpiece."

—Laura H., blogger, *Literary Focus*

"A tour de force of the lurid and macabre!"

—Will Kettington III, poet laureate

# HOW TO USE
# THE MAGICVIEW™ LENS

*"All the strength and force of man comes from his faith in things unseen."*
—James Freeman Clarke

MagicView™ offers a reading experience unlike anything you've ever seen (or haven't seen!) before.
What looks like a blank page magically fills with text and
images when the clear lens is pressed upon it.

As you read, you will use the viewer to discover clues
along with the characters. When the book describes an
action related to an illustration or image, apply the lens
to the page to reveal the character's discovery. The lens
works best in good light, and you must press firmly to see
an image clearly.

Each character is represented by a letter on the viewer.
For example, if the character Jay looks into a magic mirror,
you should turn the viewer so that "J" is at the top and
then use the lens to search the image of the mirror for
clues. If the character Brian is solving a puzzle, turn the
lens so "B" is at the top to reveal the answers.

You can see a sample of MagicView™ below. Turn the viewer so "J" is at the top and place the lens over the image below. Remember to press firmly and make sure to turn the lens to exactly the right angle. As always, for best results, read in a well-lit area.

You may notice some strobing (stripes) as you angle the viewer to see the hidden image. This means you are getting close to discovering the image. As you fine-tune the angle of the lens, the stripes will disappear, and the image will flicker into clarity with amazing detail!

# SEEING IS BELIEVING

Practice using the viewer on the image of the crystal ball on the following page. Turn and apply the viewer to see what vision each of the characters sees. Start with "J" at the top. Then turn to "P." Next turn to "D." Finally, turn to "B."

To see the images most clearly, place your fingers just inside the viewer's frame and apply equal pressure to the entire lens. You'll also want to make sure that your MagicView™ lens is right side up. (If the letters are backward, it means the viewer is upside down.)

Sometimes, more than one character will discover a clue related to the illustration. In this case, you will need to turn the viewer to the letter for each character to see what they see. For example, the character Danni might see fingerprints on a piece of paper, while the character Pam might have a psychic vision.

You must read and interpret the story to decide which character or characters are examining the images. Depending on the image, MagicView™ might reveal what just one character sees. With other images, the viewer might show what two characters see or what three characters see. Occasionally, as with the case of the crystal ball, it will show what all four characters see. On some pages, the viewer should be applied to different parts of the image for each character. Other times, the viewer should be applied to the same spot for each character.

You now know everything you need to know to uncover clues as you join our young ghost hunters on their journey through the most haunted town in America. So strap on your infrared goggles, grab your spirit boards, and open your eyes to the impossible. It's time to begin your adventure.

# CHAPTER ONE

---

# TWO AND A HALF PICTURES

Jay Winnick had two pictures of his father on his nightstand. In the first picture, his father was smiling, his arm lazily draped around Jay—then six years old—as the two posed together in front of a water park. In the second picture, his father was dead.

Not all pale and decomposing and worm-ridden—Jay wasn't a sicko—but light, airy, and ethereal: his dad's ghost. Or so Jay claimed. Anyone else who saw the picture thought the silvery blur was just a trick of light and shadow.

In the photo, sunbeams filtered through forest trees, speckling a clearing with random kaleidoscopic patterns. Although, as the now twelve-year-old Jay so often pointed out, if you squinted your eyes just right, there did appear to be the hint of a figure on a sliver of mist who looked remarkably like his dad.

Jay himself was the spitting image of the picture of his dad (the living one). He had the same dark, unruly hair, full of cowlicks and random waves. He had his dad's inquisitive, Caribbean Sea eyes, so rich in color that his mother affectionately referred to them as "illegally blue." He even had the beginning of a crease in his forehead (his father's was deep and established), borne of thought and concentration from years of reflection that most boys are spared until a much later age.

Jay kept a third picture in his nightstand drawer, taken last Fourth of July. The dim, unfocused image, shot during the fireworks' grand finale, was full of orbs—balloons of light that hovered in the sky above people's heads, below the exploding fireworks. Ghost hunters like Jay believed these orbs were the energy of spirits, while skeptics claimed that they were merely the camera flash reflected in the moisture of the air—completely explainable by science.

On the night Jay took the picture, he felt the strong presence of his father, but he couldn't be sure, not even with wishful thinking, that one of the orbs was his dad. So Jay would often say that he had two and a half pictures of his father by his bedside.

This morning, like every morning, Jay studied the pictures of his father as if committing them to memory. He did this as part of his morning routine: look at the pictures, brush his teeth, take a hurried shower, read ten pages of *Ghost Hunters Weekly*, Google new paranormal websites for twenty minutes, and then go downstairs where his mom was busy preparing a tasteless breakfast.

The reason the breakfast in question was tasteless was because Jay's mom was a worrier of professional caliber.

She had read countless articles about the health hazards of preservatives and artificial flavoring, so while other kids ate cereals full of wonderfully unnatural colors and chemically engineered marshmallowlike things, Jay ate a "natural cereal," which looked and tasted not unlike wicker.

Preparing this horrible breakfast was part of Mrs. Winnick's morning routine: wake up, worry that Jay was going to oversleep, worry if Jay was eating enough, worry if Jay was going to be late for school, worry that Jay might get in an accident on the way to school, worry about what to worry about next. Sometimes she would worry about not worrying, thinking she might be forgetting something important. Of course, if she knew how Jay actually spent his days, she'd really have something to worry about.

At school, Pam Petrucci was failing miserably once again. She stared into a teacup that sat humbly on the long, crumb-covered cafeteria table. With a deep breath, she squinted at the tea leaves, trying to bend them into some vaguely recognizable shape.

"You are uncertain," she said, her darkly lined brown eyes trained on a cluster of leaves in the corner of the cup. Although, as she said the words, she felt like she was really talking about herself, not the fourth-grade girl whose fortune she was supposedly telling.

Pam looked up at the girl's face staring icily back at her. Try as she might—and she was trying hard—to maintain

her mystic gaze, Pam blinked, and her gaze became more of a warm look, completely unsuitable for a psychic.

Pam returned her excuse for a gaze to the cup. "Um, you're thinking about one thing." She scanned the leaves desperately. "Someone or something is bothering you," she hedged.

"Uh, not really," the girl said. "I feel pretty good."

"And yet, you have a feeling of unease?" It was kind of a question this time.

"I'm feeling fine," the girl insisted.

Pam blew up at her bangs, which parted like the curtain on a theater's stage. She shifted gears. "I'm sensing a 'B,' someone with a 'B' name, someone you have feelings for…" She was stretching now. "Bo…" The girl shook her head just barely. "Bah…," Pam tried again.

The fourth grader sighed, bored.

"Buh…" Pam tried to read her expression. "Buh-yay… Bay…"

Fed up, the fourth grader finally said, "I have a crush on Robert."

"There's a 'B' in Robert. You know, in the middle."

The girl grabbed the dollar bill that lay crumpled between them on the cafeteria table. "You're not getting my money for that."

"Does he ever go by Bob?" Pam called out pathetically as the girl got up to leave.

Another unsatisfied client. And worse, Pam was counting on that money for lunch. Her frowning face stared at the one settled at the bottom of the cup, as if she was looking in a mirror. Maybe there'd be a third grader desperate enough to request her services.

"Poor Pam," Jay said, sitting down across the table in the now empty seat.

"Literally," Pam replied.

Jay held up a brown bag. "Tell you what… I'll give you what's in my lunch if you can guess what it is."

"I don't want your charity." Pam didn't need to be psychic to know what was in Jay's lunch bag. It was the same thing every day: a jelly sandwich. His mom had read about the dangers of nut allergies, so peanut butter was out of the question. Concerns about E. coli ruled out lunch meat, and "goodness knows what sort of bacteria and microvermin lurks in school cafeteria food," so Jay was left with bread and jelly every day.

"Okay, then. If you can predict what I am about to do, I'll give you my sandwich."

Pam thought for a moment. "You're going to give me your sandwich."

Jay handed her the sandwich. "Wow. How did you do that?!"

Pam's smirk softened into a smile. Then, in an instant, her expression changed. She stared, lost and longing, right through Jay like he was as ghostly as the figure in the picture on his nightstand.

Jay turned around to see what had snared Pam's interest. Brian. With a "B." And along with Brian was his girlfriend, Genevra Collins, sticking to his every move like a beautiful blond shadow.

Genevra always looked like she had just walked out of a shampoo commercial, a light breeze blowing through her lustrous hair. To Pam, Genevra looked so… *healthy*. Disgustingly healthy. Pam, on the other hand, was cursed with flat, lifeless, jet-black hair, and skin so pale that people often asked her if she was feeling okay.

"Hey, Brian," Pam said.

Brian looked toward Pam, but before he could answer, Genevra tugged at his arm and they walked away.

Pam looked into the cup and pretended to read the leaves. She called out, "You know, Genevra, I don't see you in Brian's future. Not at all, actually."

Genevra turned back and rolled her eyes at Pam. "Shut up, weirdo!"

Pam shot back to Genevra, "And I see you aging disgracefully and gaining weight in the worst of places." She held up the teacup. "The leaves don't lie."

Genevra harrumphed a sound that said, "You're so lame, I'm not even going to bother with you," then turned and clung to Brian as the school's supercouple, known to the entire student body as "Brinevra," trailed away.

"Let it go," Jay said. "I have some good news. You may earn some money today after all."

"Did we get a gig?" Pam asked.

"Yep."

"What is it?"

"I'll tell you later. Let's round up the gang after school and then we'll meet the client."

When Pam and Jay approached Danni, she didn't even notice them. She was far too engrossed in the crime scene.

She stretched her yellow police tape across the street and fastened it to an oak tree. She stared down at the victim. Blood pooled by the body, trickling into the street's gutter. Danni took out her camera and snapped a picture of the squirrel.

"Gross," Pam said, looking at the roadkill.

"I know, isn't it?" Danni agreed, unable to contain her excitement. "Check out the tire marks!" She pointed to the jagged impression that cut through the squirrel's midsection.

It was typical of Danni to find delight in things that others found gross, vile, and gagworthy, though you would never guess it by looking at her. Danni was pretty in a plain way, small—she looked two years younger than her twelve years—with angelic blond hair, which she generally wore in unusual variations of pigtails. A few lost freckles were sprinkled on her cheeks, and she was almost always smiling. Altogether, she was the picture of innocence, the last person you'd expect to be fascinated by all things steeped in gore and nastiness.

Humming pleasantly to herself, Danni placed a piece of biofoam across the mashed carcass. The foam, often used in crime-scene investigations, was engineered to make molds of footprints, but Danni realized it would work here too, so she peeled the foam back and it picked up the pattern of the tire tread imprinted on the poor animal, a perfect 3-D replica down to the last squashed squirrel gut. "I can match this to a database of tires, run some license plates, and crack this case by the weekend."

"Squirrel got hit by car," Pam said. "Case closed."

"Think so?" Danni said wryly as she stepped away from the poor creature. She backpedaled toward the side of the road where she had set down her equipment, her eyes locked on the squirrel as if at any moment it might spring to life and scamper away.

She retrieved a spray bottle from the collection of

containers, brushes, and assorted instruments by the curb and hurried back to the crime scene. She knelt down in front of the squirrel carcass and squeezed the spray bottle's trigger. A vinegar-colored mist settled onto the road.

"The aluminum oxide reacts with the rubber traces and highlights the skid marks," Danni explained as she stood up, still staring down at the road. Seconds later, two skid marks were distinctly visible.

"The skid turns toward the roadkill." Danni circled the mark in sideways steps as she spoke. "That means there was no effort to avoid the squirrel. And the skid is darkest *farther* from the squirrel. A skid mark like this suggests acceleration, not braking, meaning the driver sped up. This was no accident. This was a homicide! Or, technically, squirrelcide or… whatever."

Danni noticed something on the ground. A moment later, she was using tweezers to pick up a small hair, which she then dropped into a plastic bag.

"Really? You're going to collect hair from roadkill?" Pam asked.

"Could belong to the driver," Danni replied. "Drivers get out of the car in sixty percent of hit-and-runs."

Danni used a forensics laboratory in Albuquerque, New Mexico, to process all of her DNA testing. She only dealt with them by e-mail and she always paid her bills on time—for all they knew, she really was Lieutenant Besner of the Rockville Police. In the past two months alone, Danni had received results back from the lab confirming

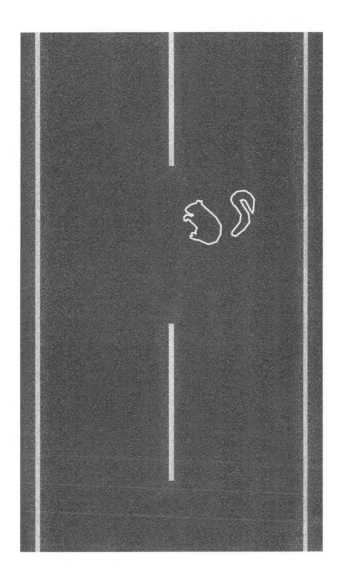

that the hairs in question were indeed those of a possum, a muskrat, and a chipmunk, respectively.

"Look at that," Danni said as she sprayed the bottle in rapid-fire bursts around the squirrel. "A footprint. The driver did get out."

She then proceeded to outline the squirrel with chalk. Unfortunately for all of those in attendance (especially the squirrel), this required her to walk several feet down the road to outline a second piece.

"Jay, you should check for ghost energy," Pam joked.

"Sorry, I draw the line at animals," Jay said.

Danni looked up from part two of the squirrel. "You never know. There's a book by M. T. Boesch called *Roadkill*." Her voice strained to keep pace with her thoughts. "It's about a squirrel that gets hit by a car, and in its last moments it memorizes the car's license plate as it drives away. Anyway, so that night, the roadkill is struck by lightning and comes back to life as a zombie squirrel with tire tracks on its body and everything, and it becomes obsessed with finding that car and hunting down its killer. I won't spoil the ending. Let's just say that a painful use of acorns is involved."

Jay was starting to get impatient. "Anyway, Danni, if you could wrap up your, uh, investigation, we have a gig to get to."

"Okay, I'm done." Danni stood up and took off her rubber gloves. "Poor thing," she said, staring down at the squirrel. "Probably just got... *tired.*"

Jay laughed despite himself. He was used to Danni's "gallows humor," the little jokes and bad puns she used to lighten up crime scenes. Danni religiously watched every crime show on TV and had quickly picked up the habit.

The three ghost hunters were on the move. Now they just needed their fourth.

Seth didn't like playing goalie. He didn't even like soccer, or sports for that matter. But his parents thought joining the team would be a good way for him to meet people in his new town. Unlike most goalies, instead of stopping the ball, Seth tried to avoid it—especially in this particular game, where Brian had been drilling shots at him with bulletlike velocity.

After the game, at precisely 4 p.m., a bruised Seth stood obediently by the monkey bars as Jay had instructed. Pam, Danni, and Jay walked toward Seth and then proceeded to walk right past him over to the other side of the field.

Seth almost said something, but as usual, he chose to stay quiet.

A lone figure sat leaning against a tree, reading the sports section of the newspaper. He held a pencil in one hand, occasionally making notes on the page.

"Game's over, Brian," Pam said. "You can drop the act."

"Is anyone still here?" Brian asked, not bothering to look up from the paper.

Jay looked around. "Just the goalie who you tenderized with your penalty shots."

"You sure?"

"Yes, we're sure," Pam said. "The coast is clear."

Brian dropped the sports page, revealing the puzzle book he had actually been reading.

"Where's *Genevra?*" Pam said the name like it was an intestinal disease.

"Cheerleading practice," Brian said.

"Thanks for saying hi today," Pam mocked.

"We talked about this," Brian said. They *had* talked about this. Many times. Brian had made it clear that he couldn't possibly be seen associating with the others at school. They were brains, and everyone knew it. But Brian was a closet brain. He went to enormous lengths to disguise his intelligence, a trait which, if discovered, would severely damage his social standing. Though he could have easily gotten straight A's, Brian worked diligently to maintain a very unimpressive C- average.

He made sure to miss enough test questions on purpose and proofread his papers so that he could add spelling mistakes at the last second. At first it pained him to miss questions he knew. But after a while, he started to have fun missing test questions in amusing ways. He just recently told his math teacher, Mrs. Fisk, that a numerator was a type of deadly robot, and claimed in history class that the Missouri Compromise was a professional basketball team.

At school, he was a tall, good-looking, simpleminded jock, which was plenty to impress girls like Genevra—and girls like Genevra were the ones Brian wanted to impress.

**Rockville Herald**

**PORTS**

## Advanced Sudoku

| | | 9 | | 5 | | | 8 | |
|---|---|---|---|---|---|---|---|---|
| 5 | 2 | | 4 | | | 6 | | 9 |
| | | | 6 | | | | | 4 |
| | | 2 | | | | | | 3 |
| | 3 | | 9 | | 8 | | | |
| 7 | | | | 3 | | | | |
| 3 | | | | 6 | | | | |
| 4 | 6 | | | 7 | | 5 | 2 | |
| 8 | | | 1 | | 3 | | | |

Answers on page 109.

But after school, it was a different story. After school, Brian was a puzzle lover, bookworm, and fellow ghost hunter.

"I'm getting a vision," Pam said, looking down at Brian. "I predict you care too much about what other people think."

"You can't just disguise your criticisms as predictions," he said.

"Oh, I predict I can."

"So what's the gig, Jay?" Danni interrupted. Her eyes lit up. "Any corpses involved?"

"Sorry," Jay said. "Maybe some minor mayhem."

"I suppose that's a start," Danni said cheerfully.

"Who's the client?" Brian asked

Jay jerked his head toward Seth.

"You gotta be kidding," Brian huffed. "What's the matter? Is he scared of his own shadow?"

"Sort of," Jay said.

# CHAPTER TWO

---

# SERVICE FOR THE NERVOUS

Jay's ghost-hunting business began as a personal quest. When he was seven, his father had mysteriously disappeared on a business trip to Philadelphia. Despite months of searching, the authorities never found him, and after a year, Michael Winnick was officially declared deceased.

Jay, who had always been a cheerful kid, became somber and withdrawn. Then, two years later, on that fateful day in the forest, he saw him. He was walking alone, deep in thought, kicking pinecones and pinching leaves off branches, when there he was.

The figure blinked in and out of the world as the clouds flirted with the sun, but Jay was sure it was his dad. He grabbed his cell phone and held it in front of him delicately—as if trying not to scare off a skittish deer. He snapped a picture of the smoky figure, the picture that would be printed and remain on his nightstand from that day on, the picture that Jay would look at every morning and every night.

He lowered the phone and took a step forward. The calmly smiling face drifted in and out of existence. Then the face changed. It looked mad, or alarmed maybe—it was hard to tell—and in an instant, the vapors thinned into floating threads, like loose spiderweb strands, and the wind blew them away.

From that moment on, Jay regained hope. He went from sad all the time to sad most of the time; and then most of the time became sometimes, which after a while turned to occasionally, until Jay was eventually once again living the energetic and laugh-filled life of a kid. This didn't mean he stopped thinking about his father. He thought about him all the time. He found every book he could about the paranormal in general and ghosts specifically. He devoured hundreds of books and thousands of websites, and checked out message boards from renowned scientists and crazy kooks alike.

He fast became an authority on ghosts, but except for that day in the woods, he had never seen one himself. Then one day Jay answered a call from a neighborhood kid on one of the message boards. She wanted help with a spirit that was haunting a tire swing over a creek near her house. Naturally, no adult believed her. But Jay knew she was telling the truth, and so he took on his first paranormal investigation. Using the latest tools that paranormal technology had to offer, Jay was able to communicate with the ghost, and he discovered that it wanted to warn the girl not to jump into the creek because it was too shallow from lack of rain. The ghost had died this very same way.

Within a year, Jay had assembled a crew and was the president of a successful after-school business. The Rockville Paranormal Investigation Corps—RPIC for short—had cleansed homes of terrifying spirits, assisted ghosts in finding their way to the Other Side from the In-Between, and opened communications between the haunter and the haunted.

Their customers consisted almost entirely of kids. In Jay's experience, adults always found ways to rationally explain what they were experiencing, and in their refusal to accept the supernatural they often suffered for longer than they had to. For those willing to employ them, however, Jay's ghost-hunting crew was providing a noble and invaluable service. They were making people's lives (and deaths) better—and bringing in a little money in the process.

But no matter how many successful investigations Jay had conducted, no matter how many cleansings and communications he had achieved, the answer to the question that had started it all still eluded him; he was no closer to finding his father. Neither the living nor the dead had been able to give him any new information about his dad. And so behind the confident and adventurous leader, behind his illegally blue eyes, there was still a deep sadness.

They followed Seth on the short walk from the soccer field to his perfectly pleasant-looking house. Seth took out a key and let himself in. The door opened to a lovely foyer with a tasteful chandelier and an unremarkable tile floor.

"Anyone else here?" Jay asked.

"Just the ghost," Seth said. "My parents are working, and my brother just started at MIT."

Seth led the way up a modern, carpeted, uncreaky, unspooky staircase. He poked his head through a door in the hallway as if he were entering a dark cave. After a moment, he sighed in relief and gestured for the others to follow him into his room.

Seth's room looked like a museum dedicated to action figures. Figures of all sizes and varieties stood, crouched, crawled, and fought, frozen and posed on his bookshelves, while stacks of comic books jutted from the floor like a sprawling city skyline.

Jay scanned the array of toys in the room until his glance landed on the Spider-Man sheets on Seth's bed. "How old are you?" Jay asked.

"Ten."

"But you're in sixth grade like the rest of us," Pam said.

"I skipped a grade."

Jay picked up a stuffed pig from the collection of animals on his bed. "You're ten? Seriously?"

Brian noticed a large chessboard on a small table. The pieces were arranged as if someone was in the middle of a game. "You play?" he asked.

"Not anymore," Seth answered. "That's not my game. It's… well, you'll see."

Brian looked at Seth, then at Jay, and raised an eyebrow. Danni, meanwhile, had already begun her crime-scene investigation. She was snapping pictures, bombarding G.I. Joes and stuffed animals with flash photography like they were celebrities on a red carpet.

Jay reached into his backpack and took out an object that resembled a remote control with a tube sticking out of it. He walked around the room, holding the tool in front of him, occasionally reading the digital numbers displayed on its small screen. He dictated into an audio recorder that he held in his other hand: "Thermal scanner shows no temperature fluctuation, no hot or cold spots whatsoever."

"Pam, you getting any *vibes*?" Brian smirked.

"I'm feeling a subtle disturbance, like some kind of negative energy—oh, wait, that's just coming from you."

Jay returned the tool to his backpack and pulled out what looked like a snorkeling mask crossed with binoculars. He strapped the goggles onto his face and looked around the room. Everything disappeared into darkness except for the orange-glowing bodies of the other people in the room. "Infrared shows nothing unusual."

He zipped up his pack and turned to Seth. "You just moved here, right?"

"Yeah."

"From Dallas?" Pam asked.

Seth looked shocked. "Yes. How'd you know that?"

She pointed to the Dallas Cowboys helmet resting in the corner of his room.

"Oh, yeah. My parents are trying to get me into sports. I'm using it as a bat cave." Closer inspection revealed a model Batmobile under the helmet.

Seth rubbed one of his many soccer-ball-size bruises. "The haunting usually begins as soon as I get home after school. Then it goes away when my mom and dad come home after work. And then it comes back at night."

A hint of a wrinkle awoke on Jay's brow. "Describe this so-called haunting."

"Well, my shelves shake. And my computer screen starts to bug out—I mean really *bug out*."

Jay dictated into his recorder: "Reported electrical disturbance. Possible object possession." He ran his fingers along the side of the monitor. "Any EVP?" he asked, turning the monitor off and then back on again.

For a moment, Seth's anxious eyes froze open in a confused stare. "Huh?"

"Electronic voice phenomena," Brian clarified. "Have you ever recorded a haunting and then heard strange sounds when you played it back?"

"EVP can indicate ghosts," Danni added as she snapped a picture of the helmet.

"I've never tried," Seth said. "I mean, I'm usually hiding under the blankets." He cast a nervous glance toward his Spider-Man pillowcase. "Well, except when my bed is…" He stopped speaking, and his eyes widened as if suddenly intimidated by the cartoonish Spider-Man staring back at him.

"What?' Jay asked. "When your bed is what?"

Seth continued staring wide-eyed and fearful at the bed. "Floating," he said.

Unfazed, Jay reached into his backpack yet again and took out a large metal box with a long antenna affixed to the top. He pointed the antenna toward the computer and waved it in front of the screen.

"What's that?" Seth asked, eyeing the device with wonder.

"Electromagnetic field detector," Jay replied. "And it's showing some activity."

"Sometimes the helmet will spin around and all my toys will start flying and—"

"Hey!" Danni interrupted from across the room. She was examining a framed picture hanging on the wall that showed Seth at an amusement park posing blissfully with a Cylon from *Battlestar Galactica*. "Look at this." She made a chalk mark on an area of the wall next to the picture. "Check out the dust pattern. This clear area is where the picture normally is; there's no dust behind where it usually hangs. But the picture has shifted…"

She took out measuring tape and stretched it from the dustless spot on the wall to where the picture currently hung. "Eight inches. Confirms object possession." She then took a picture of the picture.

"Please don't touch that," Seth pleaded to Brian, who was thumbing through a book called *Grandmaster Chess Technique.*

"Actually, we need to take this for evidence," Brian said, tucking the book in the waistband of his pants.

Jay looked around the room. He had an idea. "So, normally your so-called *ghost* comes around by now."

"What do you mean 'so-called'?" Seth asked. "It's real! But yeah, normally. I don't know why it isn't here right now."

"It's probably because you're a liar," Jay said matter-of-factly.

"Wha—?"

"A liar and a loser. You're doing this to get some attention because you have no friends."

The others looked at Jay, puzzled. Then something else grabbed their attention. Behind Seth, the shelves began to vibrate, causing the action figures to rattle and dance. A Transformer twirled like a ballerina.

Jay continued, "I mean, nobody likes you at school and people beat you up all the time. Kind of the definition of a loser."

Brian stepped in between Jay and Seth. "Jay, take it easy. You're..." He looked at Jay's eyes; then, as if understanding something, he turned around and got up in Seth's face, "...forgetting something. How about the embarrassing soccer game where everybody was watching!"

Now the shelves trembled. Action figures fell off their feet. A LEGO ship slid off its shelf, crashing to the floor.

"It's happening!" Seth turned back to the shelves and began helping his toys to their feet.

That's when the chess pieces began moving. It was as if two invisible people were playing a game. The pieces slid across the board: black then white, black then white.

As Seth panicked, Jay and the gang grew calmer. A G.I. Joe figure jumped off the bed onto Seth's head. Other figures joined the assault. Seth screamed. "Help! The ghost is here!"

He grabbed his asthma inhaler from his pocket, but before he could place it in his mouth, it squirmed out of his hand like a wriggling fish and hopped directly across the room into Pam's mouth.

"Ew, groth," Pam lisped, pulling the inhaler out of her mouth. She tossed it away, and it whizzed up to the ceiling, where it stayed stuck as if full of helium.

Seth fidgeted frantically, attempting to pry the action figures from his body. Danni took a flutter of photos of her nerdy "model," who struck pose after pose, contorting wildly in a vain effort to free himself from the toys' kung-fu-grip assault.

Meanwhile, Seth's computer screen began to flicker, and the speakers sizzled a high-pitched, staticky noise that sounded like a hundred tiny voices screaming. On-screen, the flickering swirled inward as if sucked into a digital black hole, and new images began to take shape: horrible, gruesome images, one after the next—ghosts, vampires, eyeballs, and ants—strange and terrifying visions each with its own equally terrifying sound emitting from the speakers.

Jay looked around. "Wow, this is the scariest ghost I have ever seen. Right, guys?"

Pam played along. "Yeah, there's no way we're going to be able to stop it."

The speakers screamed. The screen began to spark. The shelves continued to angrily empty their contents, and the tiny creatures continued their attack on Seth who, in the whirlwind of attacking toys and his own emotions, began to cry. Either to hide his tears from the others or to blind himself from the frightening chaos in the room, Seth closed his eyes.

Jay put his hand on Seth's shoulder. "It's okay. You don't have a ghost."

Seth opened his eyes and looked at Jay as if he was crazy.

"You have a poltergeist," Jay said.

An experienced ghost hunter like Jay knew how important it was to explain things in a calm voice. "Your emotions, your stress, all of the stuff going on inside you—that's what is projecting this energy. *You're* actually causing all of this."

Seth stared in disbelief. "But why did you—you were so mean to me!"

"Sorry about that. I needed to confirm that this was a poltergeist by exciting your emotions."

"It's called psychokinesis," Brian added.

"Psycho-what?" Seth asked.

"Psychokinesis." Brian proceeded to spell it, effortlessly in record speed: "P-s-y-c-h-o-k-i-n-e-s-i-s. A projection of

emotion manifest through energetic forces in a localized environment."

"Wait, how do you know... are you... *smart?*" It sounded like an accusation.

Brian grabbed Seth's shoulder. "Tell anyone and I'll break your face."

Seth winced; a light bulb burst by his head, and he winced again.

"Sorry," Brian said, turning to Jay.

"Here, read this." Jay took out a thick book with a dark brown leather cover. He opened the book and began rifling through its wrinkled, dog-eared pages until he got to the entry he was looking for. "Toward the bottom of the page." He handed the book to Seth, who struggled to support its weight.

The lights flickered as Seth's eyes darted nervously across the page.

"Relax," Jay said. "We can take care of it."

"What?" Seth jerked his head up from the book.

"I was hoping you'd feel better after reading that," Jay said. "Understanding what's going on and everything. But judging from the light show—"

"Those P-O-P ghosts," Seth gulped. "What if it's one of those? They sound terrifying."

"It's not one of those," Jay said, stifling a laugh. "This is a classic poltergeist. We can take care of it. I promise."

And with that, Seth—and his surroundings—finally calmed down.

Pam, on the other hand, was a little on edge. Once again, her eyes were playing tricks on her. In the margin of the page, she could have sworn she saw several words floating randomly. It was happening again! As had occurred dozens of times before, she was seeing words where there weren't any words.

The letters winked in and out of the page, twinkled like starlight, and then vanished. Pam's mother, an established and respected psychic, told Pam to ignore the words, that they were "psychic hiccups," just her "fertile imagination." Those were the terms Momma used when Pam offered an observation that wasn't steeped in solid psychic energy. So

# SERVICE FOR THE NERVOUS

**Pockets of Purgatory:** Located in caves, forests, and other unpopulated areas, pockets of purgatory (POPs) are places where the ghosts of murderers, thieves, and other such sinners are sentenced to reside, their souls having been deemed unfit for passage to the Other Side.

As penance for the hate with which they chose to live, the ghosts are cursed to feel the resentment of other similarly despicable spirits around them, inspiring in one another a constant, immeasurable anger. Because of this curse, if a mortal happens upon purgatory ghosts, he too will be beset with a hideous anger. Within minutes, the rage becomes all-consuming, the victim is frozen, and the ghost will claim its prey (see Purgatory Ghost Paralysis, page 260). The victim's soul is then trapped in the POP, doomed to eternal imprisonment surrounded by the company of his murderers.

**Poltergeist:** Though the word "poltergeist" comes from the German meaning "noisy spirit," a poltergeist is neither a spirit nor a ghost. A poltergeist is not the presence of the spirit of the deceased, but rather the result of a living person's emotional stress. If a person is experiencing powerful emotions without a proper outlet to express them, the individual's anxiety, fear, and sadness are projected into the environment. Typical poltergeist disruptions include strange noises, electrical disturbances, and objects moving about as if under their own power. The key is not to give a poltergeist fear or anxiety. If a poltergeist cannot draw off these emotions, it loses strength and eventually fades away.

**Posing:** Posing is a slang term for ghosts pretending to be living people. Most paranormal scholars believe it is a rare occurrence. However, some ghost hunters

259

each time she saw these mirages of words, Pam would just let it go and not mention it to anyone.

"So what do we do?" Seth asked, picking up his broken LEGO ship.

Jay looked around the room. Pictures swung on their nails. The chess game continued at a slower pace, and action figures strolled slowly across the carpet, like they were examining the aftermath of a hurricane. "You can see when you got distracted, the energy settled down a bit. But we need to calm you down a lot more. Luckily for you," he said, turning to Pam, "we know a very accomplished hypnotist."

Seth lay down uneasily on his levitating bed, the scars from the battle with his toys reddening into tiny bruises on his body and arms. He looked like the victim of a dozen hickeys.

"I want you to relax," Pam began in a hypnotic tone. "Breathe in. Breathe out," she continued, speaking more and more softly, her voice a soulful hum. "Picture yourself on a beach. The sun is beating down warmly on your body. You are floating on a raft in clear blue waters, bobbing ever so softly in the gentle sea. The smell of the sea salt and coconut oil…"

A fearful scowl contorted on Seth's face. On his desk, his computer screen began to flicker again, and the lights dimmed.

"Something the matter?" Pam asked.

"I can't swim!" Seth said. "And I'm afraid of the ocean. And there could be piranhas in the water."

"No," Brian interrupted. "Piranhas are river fish. Could be barracudas, though. Or a nurse shark."

Another lightbulb exploded. Pam shot Brian a dirty look.

Brian shrugged. "I'll just be over here." He pulled out the chess book and began reading.

Pam took a calming breath and began again. "Okay, you're in a forest. A cool breeze wafts through the tall trees; nearby a creek cascades down a rocky bed, the whoosh of the water singing a lullaby into the lush valley that cradles you in its soft green arms. The cool, pine-scented air fills your lungs."

All of a sudden, the picture of Seth with the Cylon turned itself around to face the wall, as if hiding the photographed Seth's eyes from the horror. The dimmed lights blinked and the action figures tap-danced.

"What now?" Pam pleaded.

"I don't like being out in the wilderness," Seth cried. "I could get mauled by a bear, and deer attacks are actually more common than you would imagine. Plus, I'm ultrasensitive to poison oak. I once used it as toilet paper when I was camping, and…" he trailed off.

"You're worse than my mom," Jay said. He grabbed the bed and pulled it down so Seth was now hovering just below shoulder height. "Where's a comfortable place for you? Where do you feel most relaxed?"

"At a Bakugan tournament."

Jay shrugged at Pam, and once again she attempted to relax Seth into a trance. In barely a whisper, she gently set the scene: "You and your fellow nerds are centered around a card table in the basement of a comic-book shop. You can feel the shiny cards, so smooth and new in your hand." She shrugged. Jay nodded, and she continued. "Each card glistens in the low light of the shop. There are no girls within miles to make you nervous. The bullies wouldn't know where to find this place…"

With each word, things in the room settled down. The lights eased back to their normal brightness, the computer screen stopped flickering, and the bed floated down to the floor. "The poltergeist is gone," Jay said, looking at the readout from his electromagnetic field detector.

Pam concluded: "When I snap my fingers, you will awaken feeling relaxed, unafraid, and ready to take on whatever new experiences life brings."

She snapped her fingers, and Seth's eyes sprung open with an expression of calm he hadn't shown in months.

Pam blew at her bangs and smiled at Seth. "Now there is the matter of payment," she said.

# CHAPTER THREE

# NOTHING TO SEE HERE

P am sat across the table watching Momma sort the mail. Pam called her mother Momma, and so did everyone else. Momma Petrucci, as she was known, was Rockville's most preeminent—and profitable—psychic.

"Bill." Momma said, putting the unopened envelope to her left. She held the next envelope to her forehead. "Invitation to a benefit."

She placed the second unopened envelope to her right. She proceeded to psychically sort the rest of the mail, not bothering to open any of it, tossing it into piles on the giant spirit board that served the dual purpose of kitchen table.

"Bill... bill..." She held one envelope for a few seconds longer than the others. "Letter from Cousin Judy going on and on about how great her kids are."

She tossed it in the trash.

"Coupons." Momma squinted, betraying just the slightest hint of concentration. "Twenty percent off an iPod nano. A hundred-dollar rebate on widescreen TVs. Darla, do you want these coupons?"

Pam's older sister, Darla, the apple of Momma's inner eye and heiress apparent in psychic ability, poked away on her cell phone, feet kicked up on the table.

"Hold on, I'm syncing my e-mails," Darla said casually.

She held the phone to her forehead just like Momma was doing with the envelopes. She rattled off the emails as they flowed from her phone into her mind as if there were a direct Bluetooth connection. "Spam… spam… Jill asking for help on the test tomorrow…"

Momma stopped sorting the mail. "Darla, you're not going to give her the answers just because you know what they'll be, are you?"

"Of course not…. I'm going to make her pay."

"That's my girl." Momma picked up the last envelope. "Huh… Here's a letter addressed to you, Pamela."

Pam grabbed the letter and began to open it.

Momma grabbed Pam's wrist. "Uh-uh. Try to see it first."

"Momma, you know I'm not good at this."

"You have to practice or you'll never develop your gift."

"Maybe I don't have a *gift*."

"Nonsense. Go on."

Pam held the letter to her forehead. She grinned and grimaced, furrowed and frowned, trying desperately to force some image to come into her mind. Nothing did.

"I'm just not getting anything," she said

"Try harder. Anything?" Momma asked.

"Nothing. My mind's totally blank."

Momma Petrucci shook her head. "Sometimes I wonder if you really are my daughter."

Pam looked up, and tears misted in her soft brown eyes, which were no match for her mom's stern, deep black stare—now that was a gaze! Pam backed her chair away from the table in a fit and hurried up to her room, where she collapsed on the bed. *Why did she have to be part of this family? If everyone at school was going to think she was a freak for being into the psychic arts, she could at least be good at it!* It wasn't fair.

At a loss, she opened the envelope and she pulled out a piece of white paper. It was blank. She turned it over to the back—also blank.

"No return address," Mrs. Winnick said, dropping the letter on the kitchen table.

Jay examined the envelope. His mom was right: There was no information about the sender—just his own name and address in a very distinguished script.

A couple of clients owed Jay money, but they knew never to send a check by mail. He couldn't risk his mom finding out about his secret enterprise. If she worried about peanut allergies and cereal, just think what she'd say if she knew he was chasing down ghosts and meddling in the affairs of the undead.

Jay tore the envelope open and pulled out a single piece of blank white paper.

"Who's it from?" his mom asked.

"I don't know. It's blank."

"What?" Mrs. Winnick grabbed the envelope from Jay. "Oh, my lord. What if it's anthrax? Or some other horrible poison!"

The next day at lunch, Pam, Danni, and Jay compared mail. The kids at the other end of the table must have thought they were crazy, staring mesmerized at blank pieces of standard copy paper.

Jay looked around the cafeteria as if searching for an answer. Instead, he found Brian looking back at him. He was sitting with the beautiful people, as usual, suffering through Genevra's interminably fascinating account of finding the perfect pair of designer sweatpants on sale. He was pretending to pay attention, but he kept looking back toward Jay, Danni, and Pam.

Once he made eye contact with Jay, Brian slyly pulled out a blank piece of paper. The three of them answered Brian with a display of their own, like lifeguards communicating with flags on a beach.

Two hours later, Jay was in science, the last class of the day. The teacher, Mr. Linkins, was lying on his back. Shirtless. On a bed of nails. With another bed of nails facedown on top of him. On top of it all was a cinder block. And next to the cinder block stood Thomas Roberge, a lanky student who had volunteered to swing a sledgehammer down onto the block.

"All for the sake of science," Mr. Linkins explained, his horn-rimmed glasses resting cockeyed on his face.

Sandwiched between the spiky boards, Mr. Linkins calmly described the purpose of the experiment. "This will demonstrate the difference between energy and momentum. When the hammer hits the block, the block will absorb the energy as it breaks. The momentum will then be spread evenly throughout the bed of nails. Because the momentum will be spread throughout the hundreds of nails, I will be perfectly fine." He paused. "That's the theory anyway."

This was par for the course in science class. Karl Xavier Linkins, who, except for his surprisingly lean, muscular physique, looked like an overgrown nerd, believed that when it came to science, seeing was believing. Rather than force his students to read a textbook and accept its dry assertions, Mr. Linkins offered up his own expertise (and body) in the name of science.

The class didn't know whether to laugh or close their eyes in anticipation of what was about to happen. Mr. Linkins took a deep breath. "Okay, go ahead, Thomas. Bring down the hammer."

Thomas had to use all of his lanky strength to raise the hammer over his head. Gravity did the rest, and the hammer thundered down on its target. The cinder block exploded in a cloud of powder and debris. There was a collective gasp. All of the students were on the edge of their seats, looking toward the cloud of powder as it settled and the air cleared. All of the students except Jay, that is. His full attention was devoted to the blank piece of paper that was hidden inside his science book the same way Brian hid his puzzles.

After a dramatic moment of silence, Mr. Linkins spoke: "In case you're wondering, I am just dandy." He tossed the top board off his chest and slowly rose from the bed of nails beneath him. "Getting up is actually the most dangerous part. You have to keep your weight evenly distributed."

He brushed some powder off his chest, revealing tiny indentations that spotted his torso. He looked like a human golf ball, covered in dimples. The bell rang and the students reluctantly got up from their desks, many of them taking time to shake Mr. Linkins's cinder-block-powder-covered hand before they left the room.

"What could be more interesting than a man possibly impaling himself with hundreds of nails?" Mr. Linkins asked, rousing Jay from his trance. He stood by Jay's desk, buttoning his plaid shirt, covering the last of the marks. "I know one thing: It's not that science book." He reached into Jay's book and pulled out the paper. "*This* is what's so fascinating?"

"Sorry," Jay said. "I think there might be something on the paper." Mr. Linkins arched an eyebrow. "Do you mind if we use the lab?" Jay asked him.

Normally, a teacher would have a whole bunch of questions: *What do you mean by "we"? Use the lab for what?*

*Why are you convinced there is something on a blank piece of paper?* However, Mr. Linkins was accustomed to Jay's unusual curiosities. He commonly offered his lab for student use, and he knew exactly who "we" was, a fact confirmed as Pam, Danni, and Brian scurried into the room from their various classes.

After school, Mr. Linkins's science room functioned as a headquarters for the four young ghost hunters. As a favor, Mr. Linkins even went along with the stories Brian had concocted to protect his popular-guy reputation. If asked why Brian was hanging around a classroom after school, Mr. Linkins would say that he had been given detention; to the beautiful people, this was a much more honorable undertaking than voluntary studying. Of course, he also preached to Brian that he should drop the dumb-jock charade, telling him that a person could be both cool and smart, as Mr. Linkins himself proved every day with his daredevil stunts.

Mr. Linkins was one of the few adults who knew about the group's paranormal investigations. He was also a proud member of the International Society of Skeptics. He told the kids that he was quite confident that the more science they were exposed to, the faster they would drop their talk of ghosts and see the world for what it really is— fully explainable by the laws of physics. For this reason, "for the sake of science," he allowed their after-school use of the room.

For Danni, the room was paradise. The supply closet

was stocked floor to ceiling with hundreds of chemicals and compounds, and the lab cabinets held all of the latest scientific equipment: microscopes, test tubes, scales, and centrifuges. It didn't take long for her to transform the room into her own forensics lab. Currently, she was dusting her seemingly blank letter with a bright orange fluorescent powder. Weeks ago, Danni had mixed the powder using the closet's supply of zinc sulfide and calcium carbonate.

"Maybe there's nothing on it," Brian said. "Maybe it's just a prank."

"You got it too," Jay pointed out. "Whoever sent this knows you're part of this. That limits it to…"

"Almost nobody. Past clients only," Brian said.

Danni grabbed one of the classroom's ultraviolet lamps and shined the beam of UV light onto the letter. "Whoa," she said, and blew softly on the paper to clear the excess powder.

"What?" Jay slid toward Danni and leaned over her shoulder. "What do you see?"

Danni grinned, a smile of discovery. "These are not normal fingerprints. There are letters in them."

"Do you think it's some kind of message?" Jay asked as Pam and Brian hunched over the piece of paper.

"Don't block the light!" Danni yelped.

She took a picture of the prints with her iPhone. Later, she'd e-mail the pictures to her lab, and if the prints were in their database (which consisted mainly of criminals), she'd have results in a few hours.

"There's got to be more to this," Jay thought out loud, looking at the paper. "The prints are at the bottom of the page. That's a weird place to put a message."

Danni nodded. "It's true. The way the prints are arranged suggests someone was holding the paper down as if writing on it." She crouched down to take a closer look. "Though it's hard to tell if the prints all belong to the same hand. I don't think they do."

Pam shook her head. "We tried black light. UV didn't show anything other than the fingerprints. Jay tried infrared goggles. What else is there?"

"Maybe there's something paranormal going on," Jay said, at a loss. "If it's from one of our past clients…"

"Hah," Mr. Linkins said, without looking up from his *National Skeptics* magazine.

Brian threw his hands up in the air. He got cranky any time a puzzle got the better of him. "We feel nothing. We see nothing. We hear nothing. What's left? Tasting it?"

Danni looked like she'd seen a ghost. (Actually, she'd seen many ghosts and had grown used to the sight. But her expression resembled that of someone who'd seen a ghost for the first time.) "That's it!" Danni said.

"You want us to eat the paper?" Brian asked

"No, smell it," she said.

Danni brought the paper close to her nose and took a big whiff, while the others looked at her as if she had lost her mind. Then, in what seemed like one breath, she spoke: "There was this M. T. Boesch short story called 'Chef

Death.' So in it there was a cookbook that had a secret ingredient for every recipe. And so the secret ingredient was written in lemon juice, which was invisible when it dried. So anyway, the secret ingredient created a chemical reaction that made the recipe lethal, and the cook-slash-murderer was making all these recipes that were killing all these people. Her calling card was to garnish the dead bodies with parsley or something, but that's not important. Anyway, no one could figure it out because they couldn't see the secret ingredient and the recipes seemed fine. The cookbook would only reveal the secret ingredient when you heated the pages."

"The acid," Brian said, as if this was the most obvious thing in the world. "The citric acid from the lemon will stay in the paper even after the juice dries and becomes undetectable. Heat would cause the acidic portions to change color."

Pam picked up a Bunsen burner.

"I don't think that's our best bet," Jay said. "We're in the wrong room."

The lower shelves in the art room were stocked with half-finished student creations: misshapen pots, first graders' hand-traced turkeys, and papier-mâché creatures so poorly constructed that they looked as if they had mutated into unknown species. One particularly unfortunate creation was a sketch of a family: The artist had started the people too low on the page, so he had to give them robot thrusters and snake bodies instead of legs. This was typical of Brian's work. Art was the one thing he was legitimately no good at. Pam had at least this one thing to hold over him: She could draw.

Unlike the rest of the room, the higher shelves were full of exquisitely crafted urns, ornate boxes, miraculous glass sculptures, elaborate jade carvings, and an assortment of other beautifully crafted masterpieces from across the globe. This was the private collection of their art teacher, Mr. Kachowski.

Mr. K, as the kids called him, often shared the histories of his ancient works of art, casually mentioning how they had come from old tombs or the private collections of long-dead kings. He never explained how exactly he had obtained these objects, however. Mr. K had a big, bushy beard, rough and gray like steel wool, and an even bigger belly that protruded and hung so far over his belt that it obscured his zipper. He wore glasses too small for his bulging head and black, scuffed boots on his wide, almost circular feet. The full effect of these features made him resemble Santa Claus after thousands of soiled chimney visits.

The photographs on the upper shelves, however, showed a very different, much younger Mr. K in action in the world's most interesting places: jungles, deserts, and rain forests. The kids were left to speculate about a thinner, more handsome, clean-shaven art collector gallivanting across the globe like Indiana Jones.

Currently, though, Mr. K was collapsed, possibly stuck,

in a chair too small for his billowing body, touching up a vase with a tiny paintbrush that was engulfed in his fat, folded hand. A palette of paints and a half-eaten Tootsie Roll sat on the table at his side.

"Why exactly do you need to use the kiln?" Mr. K asked, dabbing a spot of glaze on to the vase.

"Someone wrote us a message in lemon juice," Danni replied with an innocent smile.

"It's just for fun," Jay added. "Like a pen-pal thing."

Mr. K scrutinized them over his Santa glasses, as if deciding between naughty and nice. "Wear the gloves," he said, before returning his attention to the vase.

"Thanks, Mr. K," Jay said.

"You know," Mr. K said, rolling the vase in his hands, "the Adopo Indians, native to Papua New Guinea, would paint in citrus juices. The artist would have to wait until the midday sun to see the results. They believed the drawings had voodoo properties." He stopped painting and cricked his neck, staring off for just a moment into some distant memory.

Jay put on the art room's thick, lead-lined gloves, opened the kiln's fiery stove, and inserted the blank pages.

"All right," Danni said in her best imitation of her favorite TV detectives. "Time to... *cook the books*."

After ten minutes, Jay donned the gloves once again and reached into the kiln to retrieve the letters. As he placed the letters on the table in front of him, he was amazed at what he saw. Sure enough, writing appeared.

"I assume the fingerprints are from the librarians," Danni concluded. "Or three of the four anyway."

Mr. K continued touching up his vase. Peering up over his Santa glasses, he warned, "This may not be something you kids want to get into."

"Mr. K," Pam said, holding one of the letters up to the light, "you don't actually believe there are ghosts in the library, do you?"

Mr. K pulled at the woolly coils of his beard. "Of course not."

He scratched under his left eye. Danni immediately recognized the gesture as the action of a lying man. She had studied all the interrogation techniques from an FBI training book, and knew the top three signs someone is lying: face-scratching, raised pitch of voice, and glancing to the left and down.

"Still, it may be dangerous," Mr. K continued. "Invisible writing, private meetings: Who knows what these people are after?"

"They're librarians," Brian said. "I think we can handle them."

Mr. K returned his attention to the vase, but as the kids left the room, he spoke up again. "Be careful," he said, thoughtfully pulling at the tendrils of his beard. "Things aren't always what they seem."

# CHAPTER FOUR

## THE BOOK CASE

Jay led the way through a maze of books to the Biography section. Had the few patrons ensnared by the library's computers looked up, they would have surely noted that he knew his way around the place.

Since that fateful day in the forest, Jay had spent thousands of hours at the Rockville Public Library. For most of those hours, he was alone, his head hovering over books about ghosts and spirits until his eyes went weary and his neck grew sore. And though at first he kept to himself—he barely spoke to anyone during his research— he eventually became acquainted with the library staff, needing their help to find obscure books or uncover old, forgotten periodicals.

He was especially close with Dr. Eric Grunspan, a man of profound intelligence and unnerving vocabulary, who was something of a mentor to Jay. Dr. Grunspan, whose office was practically wallpapered with scholarly degrees—he even had a few on the ceiling—could be counted on to help Jay with what he called "a young mind's undeniable quest for knowledge."

Over the years, Dr. Grunspan agreeably dug up paranormal books and articles to encourage Jay's "hobby." When Jay confided in him about the real purpose of his studies, unlike most adults, Dr. Grunspan didn't chide him for his overactive imagination. Nor did he discourage Jay's pursuit as an exercise in inevitable disappointment. Rather, he immersed himself in Jay's quest with the conviction and discipline of an academic and the compassion of a favorite uncle.

Together, like a professor and his star student, they pored over rich, musty books that Dr. Grunspan thought might help Jay find his father again: books about communicating with ghosts, treatises on the laws of spiritual energy, and other assorted thick tomes of ghost lore. Perhaps most generous of all, Dr. Grunspan let Jay keep *The Encyclopedia of the Paranormal* for as long as he wanted. Technically, the book was four and half years overdue and Jay faced a fine of $2,248.36. But Dr. Grunspan had simply entered the book in the system as "lost," sparing Jay the unequaled wrath of librarians on the hunt for an overdue book.

"This is it," Jay said, pulling *The Biography of Robert Fulton* from the shelf.

"Shh!" Brian said, looking around nervously. "Keep your voice down."

"Yes, Jay," Pam piped up. "Keep your voice down, so people won't know that—" She raised her voice just shy of a shout. "—BRIAN NELSON IS AT THE LIBRARY!"

"*Shhhh!*" This time, Brian's "shhhh" was even louder than Pam had been.

"I wonder why they chose this book," Danni said, taking it from Jay. She turned it over in her hands, checking its dust jacket for anything unusual.

"The reason we chose that book," said a raspy voice from behind the bookshelf, "is because it is situated in a relatively sparsely attended location."

Jay caught a hint of white through the gaps in the shelves.

"In theory," the voice continued, "this would give us sufficient privacy. Of course, with the vociferousness of all your shushing, we are attracting unsolicited attention."

"Sorry?" Pam said, unsure if she was being scolded.

A moment later, Dr. Grunspan stepped out from behind the shelf. "Hello, Jay," he said with a gentle smile. He stooped to Brian's ear and whispered, almost inaudibly, "Hello, Brian."

The first thing anyone noticed about Dr. Grunspan was his hair. A white mane shot wildly from his head in all directions, like each hair was making an escape. Below the whirling wisps, his face was gaunt and kind, with silver, gleaming eyes. His clothes were simple and he wore them sloppily, as if he'd hurried to put them on. His tan tweed coat was a few sizes too big, covering a blue button-down shirt that was tucked in unevenly at his narrow waist. Wrinkled gray slacks fell just short of a pair of dusty old loafers.

Jay had never seen Dr. Grunspan in any other outfit. When he finally mustered up the gall to ask about it, Dr. Grunspan explained that he, like his idol Albert Einstein, owned thirty identical copies of his daily wardrobe. This way, men of the mind didn't have to waste thought on matters as unimportant as fashion. Dr. Grunspan liked to reserve his mental energies for deeper issues like sociology, anthropology, psycho-epistemology, and other "-ologies" with lots of prefixes, which meant they were extremely complicated and possibly useful.

"Please, come with me," Dr. Grunspan said. He turned, and the crests of his hair crashed down like cascading waves.

They followed Dr. Grunspan through the recesses of the library—far away from the other patrons—to a secluded aisle of books. At its far end, his fellow librarians awaited, huddled in the aisle's shadows.

"Thank you all for coming," Dr. Grunspan said in a very official tone. "I believe you know Professor Penfield and Miss DeHart."

As unkempt as Dr. Grunspan was, Professor Rudolph Penfield was the opposite: he was extremely…kempt. Hair tonic that smelled of another era plastered down his neatly parted gray hair and darkened it into a black, immovable mass. He wore a charcoal three-piece suit—as crisp and sharp as his temper—capped off with a purple bow tie, and his face was etched with deep wrinkles produced by eighty years of critical and cranky expression.

Agnes DeHart was stunningly beautiful. There was no need to let her hair down or take off her glasses to reveal her beauty. She looked good just as she was. Her glasses made her emerald eyes larger, and her hair, pulled back, revealed the perfect angles of her face. Many a growing boy found himself with an urgent need to locate a difficult-to-find book about some suddenly developed interest: "I'm dying to read about the Treaty of Versailles, and I just can't seem to find what I'm looking for!" Or "I'm really into the poetry of D. H. Lawrence. Perhaps you can help me find some of his love poems?"

"This is Jonathan Pross," Dr. Grunspan continued, pointing to the diminutive man to his right, who was busy pecking away at his cell phone. "He has recently been hired to digitize our rare and first-edition books."

"Hey," Pross mumbled, looking up for just a blink before returning his attention to his phone.

Jonathan Pross didn't fit in with the other librarians. He couldn't be more than a year or two out of college. He had a mobile-phone headset hooked to his ear, and the left side of his mouth curled upward—*perhaps from always speaking into the earpiece*, Danni thought as she sized him up. Whatever the reason for his peculiar lip curl, the result was a permanent smirk that made it seem like Pross was dismissing everything said and done in his presence.

Below the smirk and a flat, forgotten chin, several high-tech gadgets filled his shirt pockets and clung to his belt, making him look like a geeky cyborg.

"As you might have guessed from our letter," Dr. Grunspan continued, "we are trying to keep this matter as"—he paused, as if searching for the right word—"*inconspicuous* as possible."

"Huh?" Pam said, turning to Brian.

"Secret," Brian muttered out of the corner of his mouth.

Professor Penfield straightened his already straight tie. "Libraries are having enough trouble attracting visitors these days, with all the Wiis and widgets and whatnot."

Dr. Grunspan nodded. "Indeed. Our current ordeal could precipitate a panic and spell the end of civic participation in our hallowed halls."

Pam was about halfway through translating what Dr. Grunspan had just said, when Jonathan Pross spoke up. "All of the stuff in here will be on the Web soon enough," he squeaked, his thumbs still poking madly at his phone. "Problem is, we can't digitize the books because of the stupid ghosts."

Professor Penfield shook his head and mumbled something that sounded to Jay a lot like "dork."

Pross looked up but kept his thumbs tap-dancing on his phone. "Social media and cloud computing are where it's at, Professor. You need to stop resisting progress."

"I prefer to progress resistance," Professor Penfield

snapped back, and the deep crevices around his glaring eyes flexed like talons.

"In any case," Dr. Grunspan interjected, "at the moment, both the digitizing project and the original books themselves are in dire jeopardy." His voice became deep and imposing. "We *must* regain access."

"Did you call the authorities?" Jay asked.

"I think you know how they would respond to a reported haunting."

"Look," Professor Penfield said crankily, his cane moving about like an angry orchestra conductor's stick as he spoke. "We're librarians. We did our research. Believe me—we don't particularly like putting our fate in the dirty-fingernailed hands of a bunch of kids, but we don't have much of a choice."

Miss DeHart followed, in a tone as sweet as Penfield's was grating, "All of us have overheard others speaking gratefully of your work."

Brian flashed a smile. "Thank you, ma'am," he said in a deep voice.

Pam stifled a laugh with a fake cough.

"The old librarian adage," Dr. Grunspan added drily. "'In the silence, we hear everything…'" He paused, and they were suddenly aware of the tapping of computer keys and the flutter of turning pages. "Your accomplishments are without disputation," he continued. "And your dedication is"—he turned to Jay—"unparalleled."

"Give us a minute, please," Jay said in his most polite

voice. He gestured for his friends to follow him into the seclusion of some neighboring bookshelves, where they conspired in hushed voices.

"Should we do it?" Brian whispered. "We never take gigs from adults."

"Because they never ask us," Jay pointed out.

"I think it sounds fun," Danni said, pulling a random book from the shelf.

"What do you think, Pam?" Jay asked.

"I bet adults can pay better—like real money."

Brian laughed. "What? From all those overdue book fines?"

Pam glared at Brian under her bangs. "By the way, '*ma'am*,' Brian? Are you kidding me?"

"I was just trying to be polite," Brian insisted as Pam rolled her eyes.

"I think we should check it out," Jay said, peering though the bookshelf's gaps toward the librarians. "Dr. Grunspan has always been good to me."

One by one, the others nodded. The truth was, they were curious to see the ghosts. It had been awhile since they'd seen anything good. Poltergeists are only so exciting.

As they walked through a seemingly endless corridor of books, Jay asked his standard questions.

"Can you see through them or are they solid?"

"You can see through them," Professor Penfield said, hobbling on his cane to keep up.

Jay dictated into his recorder: "Subjects display a vaporous appearance."

"Can they touch objects?" he asked.

"Definitely," Miss DeHart said over the clacking of her heels. "They throw books—although they can pass through things too."

"Elective tactile ability," Jay said into the recorder. He slung his backpack in front of him, unzipped the front pocket, and stuffed his recorder inside. "Sounds like you're dealing with standard apparitions," he said, pulling out *The Encyclopedia of the Paranormal.*

He flipped through its crinkled pages and handed the encyclopedia to Ms. DeHart. She laid the book on a nearby desk, and the librarians huddled around it.

Pam looked down at the book over Professor Penfield's hunched shoulder. It was happening again: Words began to emerge randomly in the page's margins. They appeared silvery or somehow empty of color. Some drew themselves letter by letter into words; others flashed into being, floating there. She thought about asking Brian what the words had in common, if they were some sort of riddle, but then she thought of what Momma said: This was only a psychic hiccup, leftover debris bobbing in a polluted stream of consciousness. And yet…

"You know, if you got the e-book you wouldn't have to carry that doorstop around all the time," Pross said as Jay plopped the encyclopedia into his pack.

Professor Penfield grunted and snarled, and the pattern

of wrinkles on his face changed like a shifting maze.

Three creaking flights of stairs later, they found themselves deep in the bowels of the library. Building underground was common in Rockville. In fact, the town got its name from the limestone on which it was built. And, as any geologist can tell you, wherever there's limestone, there are caverns—and Rockville was no exception. Subsurface Rockville had everything from large tourist attractions to small caves that only locals knew about to an underground mall accessible by escalator.

There were more caves and caverns in Rockville than anywhere else in the country, and scientists believed that there were miles of them yet to be discovered. Momma Petrucci often said, "On the surface, Rockville is your average middle-class suburb. But under the surface, well, that's another story." One got the feeling from her sly smile that she was talking about more than caves.

"So, do you have any idea why the apparitions are here?" Jay asked as they continued down a narrow hall.

"It started when whiz kid over there showed up," Professor Penfield said, jabbing his cane at Jonathan Pross, who didn't notice because he was still scrolling through messages on his phone.

"You think there's a reason they're here?" Miss DeHart asked. Danni noticed that she snuck a look at Dr. Grunspan.

"There could be all sorts of reasons," Jay explained. "Revenge. Warnings. Unresolved issues with the living."

**Alectromancy:** Alectromancy is the art of divination by use of chicken. The bird is placed in a circle surrounded by letters made of birdfeed. The bird pecks at the birdfeed, indicating letters and spelling out answers to questions. Alectromancy was the inspiration for modern-day use of the spirit board.

**Apparition:** Also known as a phantom, an apparition is the disembodied soul of the deceased. Apparitions range from partially transparent to wispy and cloudlike to so realistic and solid that they are often mistaken for the living until they demonstrate a supernatural behavior (vanishing or floating to the ceiling, for example). Immune to many of Earth's natural laws, most apparitions are able to turn their ability to touch objects on and off at will. They'll knock on a door one moment, and then decide to pass through it. Though not technically alive, many apparitions, both vaporous and solid, are able to interact with the living, holding perfectly normal conversations. The reasons for their presence and interaction vary depending on the apparition. Although an apparition may haunt a location just once, others can linger for years around a particular place. In both cases, the apparition is likely to be a resident of the location or familiar with it for other reasons.

**Astral projection:** Astral projection (or astral travel) is a form of out-of-body experience (OBE) whereby the spiritual traveler departs the physical body and travels outside of it via an astral body. OBEs are said to often accompany near-death situations, though they are also attempted voluntarily in some forms of spiritual practice. Exactly what form an astral body

11

Pam turned to Professor Penfield. "Have they said anything to you?" she asked.

"Go away," Professor Penfield said curtly. And then, just before Pam was about to hurry ahead, he clarified: "They say, 'Go away.' Of course, we don't stick around long for conversation."

"Interesting." Jay thought for a moment. "They want to be heard."

At the end of the aisle, they found themselves standing before two large wooden doors. Each had an arcing bronze handle and a slit of a window that blazed white, as if the light inside was fighting to get out.

"Here we are," Dr. Grunspan said with a great deal of reverence. "The illustrious Rare Book Room."

Jay peered through the window in the door on the left. The room was a hexagonal tower, stretching from the library's foundation all the way to its top level, culminating in a domed ceiling nearly sixty feet high. Two large skylights pierced the roof, and shafts of sunbeams rayed down through the tower. Dust danced lazily in the sunlight.

Like vertical bricks holding up the room, thousands of books lined all six walls: "a tower built on knowledge," as Dr. Grunspan described it. Against the walls leaned three tall ladders, providing the only way to reach the higher shelves. The ladders were set on curved tracks at the perimeter of the room, so they could slide from one side to another. At the chamber's far end were tables cluttered with stacks of books that climbed unsteadily toward the vaulted ceiling. Most of the books had old, worn, tattered covers and yellow, time-sickened pages.

In the very center of the room, a huge machine sat like a sleeping bull. Gears, levers, mechanical arms, and a swordlike blade made it resemble something a supervillain would use in his secret lair, something he'd strap his victim into before delivering a long, drawn-out speech about all the terrible things the machine would do, giving the hero time to escape.

It reminded Danni of one of her favorite M. T. Boesch stories, about an evil villain named Conciso. Conciso learned to give very short speeches when he trapped heroes in his diabolical machines. The good guys always tried to engage him in conversation while they thought of a way out, but Conciso would have none of it. He simply turned the machine on, ending the careers (and lives) of many superheroes.

Outside the Rare Book Room, Pam shivered. Jay looked at her and immediately took out his thermal scanner. "There's a cold spot out here," he explained as the arrow on the scanner fluttered into the red zone of the temperature gauge. He turned to the librarians. "Ghosts drain and feed on energy from people and things around them. It creates what are called cold spots."

He reached into his pack and took out an object that resembled a flashlight with a series of gold coils on the end. "I'm getting excess ion readings all the way out here. There's definite ghost activity going on."

"Whoa, what is that?" Pross asked, fascinated. He reached toward the contraption.

"An ion generator." Jay jerked the device away from Pross's outstretched hand. "Watch out! Touch those coils and you'll get shocked big-time."

"Where can I buy one of those?"

Before Jay could answer, Dr. Grunspan stepped between them. "The ghosts tend to emerge when we get close to the books."

"I'm telling you," Professor Penfield grumbled, "this didn't happen until the digital doofus arrived." He shot Pross another dirty look.

"Let's see what we can find," Jay said in the awkward moment that followed.

"Be careful," Miss DeHart warned.

"Don't worry," Brian said in his manliest voice. "We'll handle this."

Pam rolled her eyes at Brian. "Really?"

Jay opened the door and crept into the sun-soaked room. Danni, Pam, and Brian followed, each stepping softly and slowly as if entering a cold pool. The doors swung shut behind them.

"There's definite EMF activity," Jay said, waving his electromagnetic field detector about the room.

Danni snapped a picture. "Got some orbs," she said. "By the stacks of books near the far wall."

Jay strapped on his infrared goggles. "Got some heat spikes too. Weird. The spikes are on the books themselves."

Meanwhile, Brian gawked in awe at this cathedral of books. There were books of every color; small books, thin books, books as big as a baking tray and as thick as Mr. K's belly. *I could live in here,* he thought. *It could be my secret lair, like Superman's Fortress of Solitude.*

Outside the room, the librarians watched through the window.

"Do you really think these kids can handle this?" Professor Penfield asked.

"They are quite capable," Dr. Grunspan replied as he looked on intently. "I have watched Jay study and mature for years."

Inside, Jay inched toward the center of the room. With each step, the EMF detector sounded: Beep… Beep… Beep. Beep. BEEP. BEEP. BEEP.

In front of him, Danni approached the massive machine. She traced her hand along a series of exposed gears the size of power saws to a large scanning bed like those commonly found on copy machines. A book lay splayed open in the tray. As she examined the machine—it was nearly as tall as she was—she couldn't help noticing a green, diamond-shaped button marked "Start." She extended her finger and aimed it at the button.

"Wait!" Jay exclaimed, but he knew it was too late.

The mechanical arms ripped open the book in the feeding tray. The blade sliced the book down the middle as if it was cutting a sandwich in half, and the machine hungrily sucked down the pages into its bowels. The digitizer in action was mesmerizing. Lights flashed, it rumbled and roared, and some hidden force spit its digested pages across the near-blinding scanning bed into a final resting tray. But as fascinating as the machine was, it wouldn't hold their attention for long.

Suddenly, several of the table's books flew open, and out burst three translucent figures. They wailed and swirled upward in wild circles.

# CHAPTER FIVE

## THE GHOST GUARD

Danni nearly fell as she ducked the dive-bombing ghost. It zipped back toward the others, who circled at the top of the tower like sharks in a tank, their ghostly mass filtering the sunbeams shining through the skylights.

"Why are you here?" Jay called out as calmly as he could under the circumstances.

"Go away!" a ghost shrieked back in a voice that sounded like shattering glass.

The ghost grabbed a ladder and sent it flying along its track toward Jay. He dove out of the way just as it *whooshed* by his head.

A second ghost began dumping books off the top shelves. They hailed down, flapping madly like geese shot in midair. Brian hopped about, dodging the falling books. Next to him, Pam grabbed a dictionary from a nearby shelf and unfolded it over her head just before a first edition *To Kill a Mockingbird* thumped off its cover.

Across the room, Jay hunkered down with Danni behind a ladder. He peered through its rungs, trying to get a look at the ghosts, but they twirled and turned too quickly for him to see them clearly. Finally, as a ghost broke from the pack and swooped down, Jay made out a mustached face amid the silver, swimming blur. The mustache was long and well-manicured, curling luxuriously at the ends.

Over the years, Jay had become well versed in fashion trends throughout history, having seen everything in ghost garb from ancient Indian headdresses to colonial three-cornered hats to 1980s ill-fitting leotards and feathered hair. *Poor '80s ghosts,* Jay often thought, *trying to be scary in acid-washed jeans and leg warmers.*

While carnival workers guessed people's ages and weights, Jay guessed ghosts' dates of death. Judging from the rich muttonchop sideburns and stovepipe hat of the second ghost, and the large, blossoming hoop dress of the third and only female ghost, these spirits died around 1865, near the end of the Civil War.

Jay reached into his backpack and pulled out a thin stick tangled with clusters of small, oval leaves. Pinning the plant under his chin, he plucked a strike-anywhere match from the bottom of his pack. He swept the match against the pack's zipper and lit the leafy end of the plant. In seconds, the sage branch ignited. Thick smoke wafted toward the vaulted ceiling.

As any decent ghost hunter knows, sage is to ghosts as garlic is to vampires. And so, not surprisingly, repulsed by the drifting sage smoke, the ghosts shot toward the far end of the room.

"Thanks, Jay," Brian muttered through his teeth as the ghosts hovered directly above him. He turned to Pam. "You don't happen to have any sage on you?" he asked, still fending off the bombardment of books from above.

"N-n-no." Pam was shivering. *The Collected Works of Fyodor Dostoyevsky Volume 1* smacked against her book helmet and ricocheted to the floor.

"All right," Brian said as *Dostoyevsky Volume 2* whizzed down, inches from his head. "Make a run for it. I'll distract them."

"Can't. I'm fr-fr-frozen."

Outside the chamber, the librarians crowded around the doors' narrow windows.

"This was a mistake," Professor Penfield said.

"Don't be so impetuous in your judgment," Dr. Grunspan replied, watching the action inside with a stoic, unblinking stare.

"But, Eric," Penfield pleaded, "they just lit a fire in a room of rare books. We need to do something."

"Not just yet."

Inside, Brian had to think fast. *The Collected Works of Dostoyevsky, Volumes 3, 4,* and *5* rained down from above—*How much did this dude write?!*—and Pam looked on the verge of collapse.

"Here, get on," he told her, grabbing one of the swinging ladders.

She stepped onto the ladder's bottom rung, which in her cold, dizzy state, felt like summiting Mount Everest. Brian took hold of the ladder, looked into her eyes, and counted, "One... two... three!" On three, he threw all of his strength behind the push. Pam sailed around the room, riding the ladder as it coasted on its track. She collapsed, tumbling to the floor by Danni and Jay.

Jay looked up at the three ghosts who blended together above him like darkening storm clouds. It felt like the blood in his body was turning solid. Goose bumps bubbled up on his skin, and he was shaking.

"What do you want?" he quavered. "How can we help you move on to the Other Side?"

"We don't want to go anywhere!" the female ghost hissed. "It's you who must leave!" And with that she swept down toward Jay and Danni, her billowing dress fluttering behind her. As she whisked by, her misty gown tickled the tops of their heads, causing their hair to stand on end with a jolt of electricity. A wind gusted in her wake, and the sage flames blew out.

The ghost touched down behind Danni, and a long, pale finger reached for her shoulder. She screamed. It felt like her skin was turning to ice. The hard, cold pain radiated from her shoulder into her back.

"Danni!" Jay yelled as he watched her cringe in pain.

With trembling fingers, he reached into his pack. He plucked a match from the bottom and pressed its head against the zipper. His hand shook violently—he wasn't sure if it was from fear or cold—and the match slipped from his finger and onto a pile of books. He gulped and reached for another match as the ghost, grimacing and angry, reeled toward him.

This time, he managed to relight the sage.

The spirit spun away from the burgeoning smoke and ducked back into the book from which it emerged. The other ghosts followed, shutting their covers behind them like cellar doors.

There was a moment of calm.

The room fell silent except for the sound of Danni's chattering teeth. Jay approached the table, sage in hand, staring at the books—deeply, intensely—as if trying to peer inside them. He swallowed and shuffled closer. He reached toward one of the covers.

All three books suddenly flew open again, and the ghosts unraveled with renewed fury. They blasted into the haze of the tower's dome.

Like a bolt of blue lightning, the mustached ghost struck down at Jay. Instinctively, he cowered, and the ghost flew right through his arm. As it passed through him, Jay felt like he'd just been stabbed with an icicle—he dropped the sage and grabbed his stinging arm. The burning branch cartwheeled onto the open book by his side.

Above him, the ghost let out a harrowing shriek that caused the shelves to shake and more books to fall off their ledges. It pulled at its own shape—gnarling, stretching, and kneading—continuing to howl in unholy cries. Confused,

Jay looked up at the ghost and then back at the book: It was on fire.

That's when it hit him. "Destroy the books!" he yelled over the din of crashing paperbacks.

Desperately, the ghost plunged toward the burning book. It feverishly tore at its pages, trying, somehow, to extinguish the flames. But it was too late. The fire quickly shrouded the ghost, who screamed and faded until he was no more.

Jay lay on the ground, weakened and stunned. He was panting, coughing to find his breath again. "We've"—he took another deep breath—"got to destroy the other books."

Brian scouted out the scene. The two remaining ghosts' books lay open on the table at the other end of the room, a mere fifteen feet away. Unfortunately, both ghosts blocked the way, floating menacingly before him.

"Do not seek that which should not be sought!" the mustached ghost commanded.

It loomed toward Brian, seeming to grow thicker, larger—moving in like a rolling fog.

Brian hoisted himself onto the ladder. As he climbed, the ghost descended, and he found himself staring directly into its vacant eyes. They filled with a malicious boil, and the ghost lunged. At the last second, Brian pushed off the edge of the shelf and flung himself around the room, circling away from the ghosts toward the open books.

Meanwhile, the ghost woman clutched Danni by the shoulders. It picked her up, like a hawk seizing a field mouse, and flung her down on the digitizer. She squirmed and clawed at her captor, but her hands passed through the apparition. She found herself lying against the machine's paper-feeding tray, the blade poised above her neck. The machine hummed to life. There would be no supervillain speech.

The mechanical arms clamped onto Danni's shirt and tore off the sleeves. The ghost soared away as the blade came crashing down. She turned her head—and was suddenly blinded by bright light. *Is this it? Is this the white light you see when you go to the Other Side?* On the machine's monitor, her face appeared, frozen in horror. She had just been digitized… but she had managed to roll away in time. The blade had missed her.

"Danni, catch!" Brian yelped, heaving a book over the machine.

The book's momentum nearly knocked her over, but Danni caught it and knew exactly what to do. She placed the book open-faced in the feeding tray. She hit the start button, and the blade sliced the book in half. The two robotic arms yanked the cover of the book from its interior, and the pages were sucked toward the scanning bed.

The ghost screamed. Her vaporous body began to shred into pieces, smaller and smaller, until it was just white confetti that drifted down and disappeared before it hit the floor like windblown snow flurries.

"Fools!" the last ghost bellowed. "Things are lost so as not to be found!"

The apparition opened its mouth and a dark void gaped beneath its nose. It was as if the ghost was swallowing itself. The void grew and stretched unnaturally, as an icy blast of air hit Jay from behind like a brick wall, freezing him in place. The ghost descended, about to claim its prey, when it shrieked in horror and tumbled wildly into a backstop of books.

Pam stood by the digitizer. As the machine tortured the third book, the ghost wailed in agony. Its shape dissipated, and it smoked about the room like the last desperate puffs from a pipe.

"So they're gone?" Dr. Grunspan asked, tiptoeing through the rubble of books on the floor.

"At what cost?" Professor Penfield said pointedly, examining a battered book cover. "Rare books damaged. First editions destroyed." He picked up a blackened scrap. "Entire volumes burned!"

Jay scanned the room. It looked like a tornado had touched down. The shelves were half-full at best. Piles of books lay heaped on the floor like paper igloos. Professor Penfield groaned as he bent over and gently caressed a fallen book with the back of his hand.

Pam gave the professor a nervous look. "I'm afraid you will have to pay for any damage yourselves," she said. "It's part of the standard Acts of Supernatural Beings clause in our agreement."

Jonathan Pross rushed to the digitizer, nearly knocking

Danni down in the process. He placed his hands on the machine as if it were a wounded animal. He let out a sigh of relief: "She's still functional."

"Make yourself useful and start stacking," Professor Penfield belted. He threw a book at Pross with surprising force. "So what happened, exactly?" he rumbled, hoisting himself upright with his cane. "You destroyed the books and the ghosts just vanished? That's it?" He crinkled his nose at Jay, who felt like he was at school being pop-quizzed.

"They were bound to the books," Jay explained. "It's called tethering."

"Go on," Dr. Grunspan encouraged.

"Ghosts are tethered to things," Jay continued. "Usually it's a place. Where they lived. Where they died. These ghosts were tethered to objects, to the books. So when we destroyed the books, we destroyed their connection to our world."

"Why were they tethered to the books?" Miss DeHart asked.

"I don't know." Jay shrugged. "A curse maybe? It seems like they were protecting something."

"And what exactly were they protecting?" Professor Penfield challenged.

"Any further investigation will cost you a supplemental fee," Pam quickly slipped in.

Dr. Grunspan straightened a stack of books on a table. "I'm afraid that the public library's resources are not especially copious."

Pam shot a quizzical look at Brian.

"They're poor," he said.

Jay looked at Dr. Grunspan. His gentle eyes flitted about the walls of the room, and as Jay watched him, he got the sense of a man who had just seen his home destroyed. His world and, to some extent, his very existence had been threatened.

"We can look into it for you," Jay said, to Pam's surprise.

After the librarians left, Danni examined every nook of the Rare Book Room. She dusted for fingerprints. She tested for electromagnetic disturbance. She climbed the ladders so she could take overhead photos of the scene. She confirmed the obvious: There were ghosts in this room who were intent on keeping people out. But she discovered something not so obvious as well.

# CHAPTER SIX

# BOARD TO DEATH

"**S**omebody was looking for something," Danni said. "These books have been taken off the shelves and stacked. It's as if someone was taking the time to go through them one by one."

"The ghosts?" Brian suggested.

"No." Danni shook her head. "The ghosts were far more careless in the way they were tossing books around. Plus, I'm getting fingerprints on these."

"Can you identify them?" Jay asked.

"Well, they match one of the prints on the letter. The one that didn't have a letter in it."

"One of the librarians," Brian thought out loud. "But which one?"

Danni shrugged. "Dunno. The database didn't have the print."

Jay looked down at the massacre of books, then up

at the towering shelves that encircled them. The glare through the skylights caused him to squint. "I think we've done everything we can do here, Danni," he said. "It's time to take a different tack." He turned to Pam, who rolled her dark eyes in reluctant acceptance of what was to come.

The four ghost hunters gathered around the Petruccis' spirit board kitchen table. For six generations, the Petruccis had used the table/board (hewn from a lightning-struck hazel tree) to conjure spirit energies, portend the future, and eat scrambled eggs on. Most famously, Momma Petrucci used the table to predict the Rockville Earthquake of 1998, and for a "more-than-fair" price, as she reminded the mayor often.

Darla used the table for less important purposes, such as foreseeing what her classmates would be wearing to school the next day so that she could avoid wearing the same thing. Pam could only wonder what the spirits were thinking when they were asked such momentous questions as, "Tell me, forces of the Great Beyond, which belt will Lauren be rocking tomorrow?"

Meanwhile, Pam had had little success with the board, and she made this quite clear to the others.

"I'm not making any promises," she said as she slid the planchette onto the board. (The planchette, a heart-shaped piece of glass, was the tool that spirits used to guide mortals' hands to letters on the board.)

Pam closed her eyes. And then immediately opened them. "And you have to understand that the way this works with me is sometimes the letters don't come out in order, so you have to unscramble them."

"Cool, anagrams!" Brian said excitedly.

"Yeah, totally cool," Pam mocked, before closing her eyes again.

She struggled to settle into a trance state as Darla yapped away on the phone in the next room: "Yes, I know exactly what questions will be on the test... I had a vision in my dream last night... I have several packages available. For sections one to three, it's twenty-five dollars. For the whole test, it's fifty dollars."

"Atta girl!" Momma hollered proudly from upstairs.

*Couldn't Momma just have complimented Darla psychically,* thought Pam, *instead of ruining my concentration?* Frazzled, she shook out her arms, closed her eyes yet again, and took three deep breaths. Then, in a low, steady voice, she growled, "Spirits of the Great Beyond, fill me with your energy. Guide my hand and move my heart. Tell me what it is the ghosts were protecting."

At first, nothing happened. Then, like a butterfly coming to life, the planchette trembled just a bit. It slid slowly across the board until it stopped on a letter. Pam's eyelashes fluttered as if she was seeing something behind her closed lids, and her hands began to move again. The planchette slid to a second letter, then to a third. And that was it.

She felt proud. Usually, the planchette just sat still, like a sleeping turtle on a rock, but this time it had actually

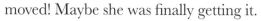

moved! Maybe she was finally getting it.

"Are you kidding?!" Brian laughed.

"What does it mean?" Danni asked.

"If you unscramble the letters, you get 'Pam.' That's what." He shot Pam a mocking glance. "Congratulations. You just spelled your name!"

Pam was furious, but Brian was right, so she said the only sensible thing she could think of in this situation: "Shut up, Brian!" Then she added to the group, "I told you not to expect anything."

"I'm sure you'll get it eventually, Pam," Jay said. "For now, though, why don't we call your sister in here. Tell her we'll give her ten bucks for two minutes of her time."

"Your name?" Darla snickered, as she joined them at the table. "That's worse than no movement at all."

"Just talk to the stupid spirits and get us our answer," Pam snapped.

"I need to use somebody who was in the library. Somebody who felt the spirits' energy. I need to guide their hands to—"

"I'll do it," Brian said before Darla had even finished her sentence. "I practically touched them and everything."

Darla looked a lot like Pam, but she was older and had grown into her distinctive Petrucci features. Her style of dress and goth makeup made her look mysterious and exotic, whereas with Pam, it almost seemed like she was wearing a costume, one she wanted to tear off right after

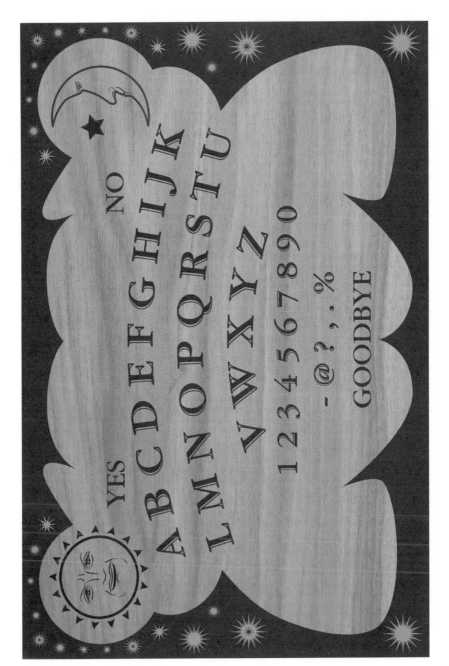

she washed the black eyeliner off her face. But as Momma always said, a psychic had to look the part.

Darla took hold of Brian's hand, and Pam nearly hurled all over the spirit board. *Maybe Darla could read the barf chunks like tea leaves*, she thought as her big sister closed her eyes. Soon, Darla's hand and, with it, Brian's began to slide on the board, settling on the number 2. They then moved to the 0.

"Twenty? What does that mean?" Jay asked, mystified. "They're searching for the number twenty?"

"Oh, I'm sorry, I was just letting the spirits determine the proper price for my services."

Jay shook his head and tossed another ten-dollar bill on the table.

"Okay, here we go. Watch and learn, Pam." Darla closed her eyes. Suddenly, it was like there was a wall of glass and shadow between her and the rest of the world. The lights dimmed in deference. Her voice fell two pitches lower than normal and she spoke: "Spirits of the Great Beyond, come forth to me. Fill our bodies and guide our hands."

This time, the planchette slid speedily with sharp, angled turns—it was like watching an air-hockey puck skim across a table—before settling on a series of numbers and letters.

Darla opened her eyes and casually shook off her trance like someone shaking out the cobwebs after a long nap. She grabbed the money and left the room without saying another word.

"What does it mean?" Pam asked, following her sister out of the kitchen.

"I have no idea. That's all the spirits gave me." She looked at Pam with the slimmest of smiles. "You know, Brian *is* cute."

"You didn't need his hand, did you?" Pam whispered with such anger that it wasn't really a whisper.

"Relax, Pam. I'm not after Brian. He's a little young for me. Besides, I can see the two of you together."

"What?"

"I gotta go. Julie's about to call." Darla's cell phone rang. "Hey, Jules."

"Wait," Pam said, grabbing Darla's phone and covering the mouthpiece. "You mean you can see us together? Like, you think we make a good match or, like, you can *see* us together like you had a psychic vision?"

Darla looked at her little sister's pleading face. "Pam, some things are better left unknown." She barely smiled, and, for just a moment, Darla didn't look so mysterious.

Brian sat staring at a piece of paper so full of scrawl and scribbles that there was hardly any white space left at all. Below "E245.7," the letters and numbers that Darla had "found," he'd jotted down dozens of ideas about what they could be: a phone number, GPS coordinates, maybe even an acrostic or secret code.

"I'm not finding anything online," Danni said, a laptop open in front of her.

Brian continued to stare at the numbers. His pinkie finger scratched back and forth across his eyebrow, something he did when he was trying to figure things out.

"Maybe it's in the EP," Jay opened up *The Encyclopedia of the Paranormal* and flipped through the pages, looking randomly for any mention of the sequence. "I can see why they want to digitize the books. We'd be able to search way more quickly."

After a few minutes, Jay tossed the book down in frustration, and it crashed onto the spirit board.

"Jay, watch it!" Pam said. "That thing's been in my family for seven generations. They'll kill me if it gets the slightest scratch." She picked up the book and checked the table for damage. "When I spilled my orange juice on it, I was grounded for a week! Fortunately, Darla read the spill to predict a stock market drop, or it would have been much longer."

Pam started to hand the book back to Jay when something on its spine caught her eye. "Bingo," she said, not letting go of the book as Jay grasped it.

"Bingo?" Danni said, utterly confused. "Like a bingo number?"

"I know what the code is," Pam said, and she pointed to the small white strip on the side of the book. "Look at the spine."

"The sequence is a library label," Brian realized, upset. How could Pam, of all people, have beaten him to the answer?!

"How exactly did you get this information?" Miss DeHart asked when they returned to the library the following day.

Jay handed her the scrap of paper with the book number. "We have to—um—protect our sources."

Miss DeHart let her piercing stare linger on Jay before nodding politely and turning to the computer on the library's counter. "Let's see what we can find."

"Are the other librarians here?" Jay asked.

"They're occupied." Miss DeHart glanced at the scrap of paper, tapped a few keys, and then fell silent, staring into the screen.

"Did you find it?" Jay asked.

She paused and then said only, "Yes."

"Well, what is it?"

Again, she was slow to speak. "It's a book called *The Dominion Glass*," she said. The sheen from the monitor reflected in her glasses as she read. "It's housed in the Rare Book Room."

"Makes sense," Brian said. "That's where the ghosts were."

"Have you heard of it?" Jay asked her.

"I'm a librarian," Miss DeHart said. "Of course I've heard of it."

Danni tried to gauge her expression to tell if she was joking, but Miss DeHart's bespectacled eyes were like frozen ponds on a sunny day, both murky and bright, and impossible to decipher.

"Well, then," Miss DeHart said, easing gracefully as always around the counter. "Shall we?"

Unfortunately, the book wasn't anywhere near where it should have been. None of the books were.

"I noticed this yesterday," Danni explained. "The ghosts must have mixed all the books up so it'd be hard to find."

"I'm afraid you're right," Miss DeHart agreed, her eyes bobbing along a row of books. She turned from the shelves and surveyed the literary mishmash still heaped on the floor. "I suppose I should relay this information to the other librarians. In the meantime," she continued, "you can start looking for the book." She looked around and sighed. "It may take awhile."

"Right," Jay said, gazing up at the towering walls of books. The tops of the shelves vanished in the light above like mountain peaks lost in clouds.

"If you find the book before I return, please bring it to me." Miss DeHart smiled, but it was a tense and serious smile. "Immediately."

"Is it important?" Brian asked. "Is it worth a lot or something?"

"You could say that," she answered. Then she turned and pushed through the massive wooden doors, the clacking of her heels silenced as the doors slammed shut.

"Do we have to go through all of these?" Brian whined.

The massive collection of books that was so inspiring

a day ago now seemed daunting. Brian preferred solving puzzles with logic, not through trial and error. Jay, on the other hand, was accustomed to long, endless searches, and was capable of obsessive dedication to a degree far beyond that of most adults. The others could tell that he was dead set on finding the book. They saw that familiar look in his eye, the unbreakable focus he'd display whenever he set his mind to a task.

And so, under Jay's command, they began sorting through the avalanche of books—some with boring titles (*The Wisconsin State Budget 1882*) and some with fascinating ones (*Werewolves: Legends of the Wild*). Danni found a forensics book called *Gunshot Wounds: A Visual Guide*, which she spent ten minutes reading, fighting off a smile as she flipped through its gory pages. Brian found a book on ancient puzzles that he decided he'd "need as evidence." Meanwhile, Pam closed her eyes and wandered around, hoping she'd feel the book's location and be drawn to it. Instead, she rambled aimlessly like a disoriented child playing Pin the Tail on the Donkey, tripped over a pile of books, and was promptly drawn to the floor.

Even Jay, despite thousands of hours spent in the library, stumbled across some books concerning the paranormal that he never knew existed. *Corpses, Coffins, and Crypts* discussed the different burial techniques across cultures throughout history. Browsing through its pages, he learned that Egyptian mummification took seventy-five days and involved removing the internal organs and placing them in jars. When he explained to Danni that they removed the brain through the nose, she was delighted and tore the book from his hands to check out the pictures.

After two hours full of paper cuts and dusty sneezes, Jay broke the silence. "I think I found it," he said with tired excitement. He wiped his blue, bloodshot eyes and checked the book label to be sure. It was a tall, thin book, with a red leather cover embossed with gold writing: *The Dominion Glass*, by Ivan Warga. Four gold clasps ran down the edge of the book, buckling it shut. Jay was about to unlatch the first clasp when he heard a high-pitched voice.

"Super," Jonathan Pross snorted.

Jay turned to find Pross standing in the doorway, spotlit by a shaft of light. "I'll take it to the others." He walked toward Jay and extended his hand.

Jay scanned Pross's lopsided face. Something told him this wasn't right. At the same time, Danni noticed that Pross was blinking rapidly and that he'd looked down to the left when he mentioned taking the book to the others.

"We'll take it to them ourselves," Jay said coldly.

"No need. I can do that."

"Just the same, we'd like to—"

And that's when Pross pulled out a very unusual gun.

## CHAPTER SEVEN

# BATTLE IN THE BOOK ROOM

The gun was black and snub-nosed. Electric purple streaks wriggled ominously at the barrel's brim.

"This is an M26 Taser," Pross sneered. "I know it looks small, but this little beauty packs over fifty thousand volts." He beamed an uneven grin. "And in case you're wondering, it has a reach of over twenty feet."

Jay tried to gauge their distance from the gun.

"I'll save you the math," Pross said. "You're well within range." He turned to admire the weapon, and the purple scars of light reflected in his beady eyes. "You know, you should feel privileged to be threatened by such a technological masterpiece. The electrical wave will find any organic matter in its path, which means I can take all four of you out with just one squeeze of this trigger. And best of all, it's as quiet as…" His smirk crawled a good inch up his cheek. "…a library." This is where they expected a maniacal laugh, the heavy, hacking kind that only evildoers are capable of when revealing the genius of their schemes. But instead, Pross just stared at them and said quite plainly, "LOL."

Jay's eyes glared a severe, stormy blue, and for a second, he thought about jumping Pross. But he held back; he didn't want to endanger his friends.

"Now, if you don't mind, I'll take that waste of tree pulp off your hands." Pross took a step toward his captives.

"Don't give it to him, Jay," Danni exclaimed.

Pross turned the gun to Danni. He lightly squeezed the trigger, and the electric strands sparked silently inches from the gun's nose, tickling the air in a deadly tease. Reluctantly, Jay tossed Pross the book, which he caught in his open hand.

"T-H-X," Pross smirked. Then, keeping his hand on the gun and an eye on his captives, he hurried over to the digitizer.

He set the book down in the machine's feeding tray and pressed the start button. Within moments, a scanned version of the book had been created. The original book lay unbound and bisected in the digitizer out-tray. The cover had been severed from its pages, but otherwise the book had survived. Still holding the gun, Pross masterfully pecked away at the digitizer's computer keyboard with his free hand.

"Why do you want the book?" Jay demanded.

"*Book?* I have no need for something as obsolete as a *book*." Pross said "book" as if it was a dirty word. "I want its *content*. I want *information*." He finished typing on the keyboard and pulled out his phone. "The entire contents of that book are now on my cell phone." He turned the phone toward them. The *Dominion Glass* cover appeared on the phone's screen. "Far more environmentally friendly, wouldn't you say?"

Not waiting for an answer, he continued, "Just one thing left to do." He stooped to the floor and rummaged through a pile of books. When he stood upright again, he held a match between his thumb and forefinger. "You know, you really should clean up after yourself," he told Jay, his beady eyes twinkling.

Pross leaned over the scanning bed and struck the match against the *Dominion Glass* cover. He seemed to delight in watching its flame dance over the loose pages, lying helpless before him. "Oh, paper," he said, smugly. "So quaint. So yesterday. So... *flammable.*"

He was about to drop the match when... *smack!* A sliding ladder knocked into his side, barreling him to the ground. His wrist banged hard against the shelf behind him, and the Taser leaped from his hand. The match, still lit, helicoptered down to a collage of books strewn about the floor.

On the other side of the room, by the two large open doors, stood Dr. Grunspan, looking very, very angry. Miss DeHart stepped out from the shadows behind him, her glasses magnifying a steely stare.

Pross gathered his bearings and reached for the Taser— when out of nowhere, a figure flipped, twirled, tumbled, and vaulted across the floor. When the movement stopped, the blur revealed itself to be none other than Professor Penfield—all eighty-plus years of him—who concluded his acrobatics with a roundhouse kick to Pross's tiny jaw.

Behind him, the books on the floor had caught fire, and the blaze was spreading fast. The four young ghost hunters just stood there—shocked still—as the swirl of limbs and madness ensued.

Pross plunged his fist toward Penfield's ribs, but the professor turned, avoiding the punch. He grabbed Pross's arm, twisted it, and drove it down so that Pross was soon on his knees. Then, seamlessly, the old man released Pross, dove over a wall of flame, somersaulted to the digitizer, and plucked the loose pages of *The Dominion Glass* away from the encroaching fire. His wrinkles, reddened by the firelight, gleamed like war paint.

Meanwhile, Pross got to his feet just in time to find Dr. Grunspan and Miss DeHart creeping toward him. The room was now spotted with bonfires. The smoke thickened. Tiny curls of singed paper drifted up from the floor and filled the air, hovering like fireflies.

"Hand it over!" Dr. Grunspan roared more loudly than Jay had ever heard the gentle man speak.

"Hand what over?" Pross replied. "I have none of your books."

"Digital or not, that is the property of the library." Grunspan stepped toward him, seemingly undeterred by the fire all around him.

Pross reached down, grabbed a book that was partially on fire, and hurled it at Dr. Grunspan. It streaked across the room like a comet. With the slightest motion—it looked like he had barely moved at all—Dr. Grunspan dodged the book.

Jay watched, still frozen in fear and confusion, as Pross took advantage of the moment to reach for the Taser. The flames between Pross and the librarians were waist-high now, a fiery picket fence dividing the room. Plumes of smoke billowed from the burning books, blotting out the skylights. Dense and silver, the twisting smoke seemed alive, and Jay swore he saw shapes and the faint hint of faces, as if the characters and stories in the books were emerging from the swirling smoke.

A few feet away, Pam, Brian, and Danni watched helplessly as flaming patches of books began to connect, separating them from Jay and cutting off any means of escape. Miss DeHart, however, was unfazed. High heels and all, she skipped over the flames, disappearing into a cloud of smoke. Seconds later, a sharp heel emerged from the cloud, spearing Pross's chest. He recoiled and dropped the Taser.

"The books!" Professor Penfield yelled. "Save them!" He hopscotched over to a fire extinguisher and wrenched it from its fixture.

Jay fanned the smoke from his face. On the near wall, he spied a fire alarm. He covered his mouth and rushed to pull it.

"No," Dr. Grunspan said, grabbing his hand. "The sprinklers will ruin the books."

"But—"

Dr. Grunspan pulled Jay's arm away from the lever.

Miss DeHart turned away from Pross and focused her attention on the spreading fire. She gracefully danced around pockets of flame and plucked unscathed books from the fiery floor.

As Professor Penfield let loose with the fire extinguisher, and the geyser of foam mixed with flame and smoke, Jay could barely make out Pross darting from the room. Jay looked back at the three librarians desperately trying to quell the fire, dousing the flames surrounding his friends. Watching Professor Penfield nimbly skirt across the room, rescuing books, braving the wildfire, Jay had the sneaking suspicion that these were no ordinary librarians.

# CHAPTER EIGHT

# THE ASSOCIATION

Hundreds of books lay splayed open and half-charred on the floor.

Professor Penfield scuttled about, his cane hooked uselessly on the rung of a ladder. With a deep sigh, he bent down and gently touched a book as if feeling for the pulse of a fallen soldier. Dr. Grunspan cradled the pages of *The Dominion Glass* in his arms as he blew the soot from a smoldering paperback. Next to him, Miss DeHart pinned back her hair, and her eyes shone with an intensity the young ghost hunters had never noticed before. The three librarians converged by the tables at the far end of the room and began whispering to one another.

From across the room, Danni tried to read their lips. She practiced this skill regularly since any forensics detective worth her salt needed to be able to do so when reviewing silent security tape footage. As she made out Professor Penfield's crinkled lips distinctly mouth the words "secret will be exposed," she mumbled, "I guess they really care about their books."

"Somebody needs to ask them who they are," Brian said, turning to Jay expectantly.

Jay got the sense that the librarians didn't want to be interrupted, much less pestered with questions. But, considering that he and his friends had almost died twice—first by Taser, and now by fire—he felt they were entitled to some sort of an explanation. He nodded and slowly made his approach.

"Um, excuse me," he said. "How did—" He tried again: "What was—" This was weird. He wasn't used to being tongue-tied. Finally, he just blurted out, "Who *are* you people?"

He wouldn't get his answer, at least not today. The librarians, or whoever they really were, insisted that the kids go home.

"For your own protection," Miss DeHart said.

"We'll contact you if and when we see fit," Professor Penfield added tersely, and they were ushered out and told, in a grave and official tone, to keep the day's events to themselves—no matter what.

That night, Jay slept little, fitfully spinning through half-awake dreams of the book room's battle, of Miss DeHart's piercing combat stare, of tumbling eighty-year-olds. Then his dreams dimmed and dissolved into something new, and Jay found himself with his father.

The two of them were making model airplanes. It used to be Jay's favorite thing in the world. They'd work together for hours, mostly in silence, because nothing needed to be said. It was just an excuse to be together. In the dream, Jay felt a happiness that he hadn't felt in his waking life for a long time. But then his dad put on a pilot's hat, and the ceiling of their home opened up, a glassless version of the skylights in the Rare Book Room. His father floated up and out of the opening and was lost in the light above.

**XL259:**

Are you there?

**GeeKing:**

Y

**XL259:**

Bceause I wsant to alk to yoiu.

**GeeKing:**

Y MEANS "YES" NOT "WHY"

**XL259:**

Do yuo havbe the boopk secure?

**GeeKing:**

Y WILL BGIN 2MORO

**XL259:**

Do nopt wastt timne

**GeeKing:**

RLX. WILL B K

**XL259:**

What does K meabn?

**GeeKing:**
> OK.

**XL259:**
> You can"t tpye "OK?"

**GeeKing:**
> GTG.

**XL259:**
> Huh?

**GeeKing:**
> GOT TO GO.

**XL259:**
> If you wanmt your money, gte the gLASS quicklty!

**GeeKing:**
> K ;)

The next day, Jay was so tired from his poor night of sleep that he hardly noticed the piece of paper fall out of his math book when he pulled it from his locker. The paper was blank.

"These so-called librarians are sneaky," Pam said as Jay showed her the paper before lunch. "I mean, how did they get this into your locker?"

"I have no idea."

All four ghost hunters finished their lunches as quickly as possible, each gobbling down a half-dozen Tater Tots and a piece of pale pizza topped with boogerlike sausage clumps, and, in Jay's case, a jelly sandwich and a packet of dried fruit from which all moisture and taste had been sucked out. They darted to Mr. Kachowski's art room and found him wedged behind a table, dusting an exquisitely carved jade swan. Candy wrappers were strewn all over his workspace.

"You certainly have a strange pen pal," Mr. K said as they placed the letter in the kiln.

"It's just, uh, for a game," Jay lied, scratching his chin.

"Yeah, it's call LARPing," Brian added quickly. "For 'Live-Action Role Playing'—I mean, I'm not playing, but these guys…"

Mr. K blew on the swan's neck and wiped it with the tent of a smock that hung over his monstrous belly. "You know," he said, turning the swan over in his hands, "nomadic aboriginal tribes have their own version of pen pals." Behind his glasses, he smiled just barely in the eyes, and continued, "A tribal chief will scrawl a message on a scrap of bark and spear it to a designated tree branch for another chief to find." He set the swan down on the table (atop a nest of empty Butterfinger wrappers), and stared dreamily into the jade. "Of course, they write in blood."

"Cool," Danni said, though judging from the looks on the others' faces, she was the only one who thought so.

After a few minutes, Jay put on the protective gloves and retrieved the paper from the kiln. Once again, writing had appeared.

They huddled around the note and squinted to read the faint script. Not surprisingly, Brian finished reading

first, as evidenced by his looking back over his shoulder at Mr. K, whose attention was once again snared by the magnificent swan.

"Well, when they say it like that, how can we refuse?" Pam said slyly just before the bell rang.

At least we might actually get some answers," Brian added with a shrug.

"We better get to class," Jay said as the writing twinkled away like stars lost at sunrise. "We'll meet up after school."

As they left the art room, Mr. K called out to them. "Enjoy your LARPing," he said with a guttural chuckle, and then his mouth closed for the briefest of moments before it opened again to welcome a handful of Hershey's Kisses.

That afternoon, the ghost hunters went directly from school to the Rockville Public Library.

The Rare Book Room was still in disarray. A half-dozen carts were overloaded with books—they were bound tight with bungee cords—and the shelves were now more empty than full. On the tables, badly damaged books were propped open under desk lamps like patients on life support in the ER. Next to them was an assortment of bottles, sprays, and small brushes, while still other books, burned beyond recognition, were clustered together in bins. The entire room had the feel of a makeshift hospital thrown together at the site of a natural disaster.

Danni turned to Miss DeHart. "Are you going to be able to repair—"

"*Shh!*" Miss DeHart said sharply. It was the first normal thing any of the mysterious bookworms had said or done in a while. *Maybe they were just librarians,* Jay thought.

"We'll talk in the secret chamber," Miss DeHart said.

*Then again,* Jay thought, *maybe not.*

Dr. Grunspan nodded and walked over to the far wall. He pulled a book from the shelf. Professor Penfield, moving perfectly fine without his cane, removed another book from a shelf across the room. Miss DeHart bent down to the bottom shelf and retrieved a third book.

A click echoed throughout the room. Dr. Grunspan leaned into a bookshelf, and it swung open, revealing a hidden chamber.

"It's a combination lock," Dr. Grunspan explained. "Three of our most uninteresting books—books no one would check out alone, much less in combination."

Jay looked at the books that the librarians had selected: *Slugs: Classifications and Considerations; A History of Doorknobs;* and *The Use of Vegetables as Symbolism in 18th-Century British Literature.*

The librarians entered the hidden room, and the others followed. Miss DeHart swiveled the bookshelf closed, eclipsing the light shining down from the skylights above. After a few steps in darkness, Professor Penfield flipped a switch, and a series of lanterns buzzed alive, bathing the room in a soft orange glow.

The secret chamber was about half the diameter of the Rare Book Room, but it felt much smaller. Its ceiling was low and uneven, carved out of the natural limestone at the library's foundation. There were nooks and alcoves and pockets lost in darkness. Strange contraptions were scattered about: swinging pendulums, rusty mirrors, a coiled wooden screw, old globes, massive hourglasses, and all sorts of mechanisms with springs and levers and pulleys and windups. The room reminded Brian of the time he skipped soccer practice (he had faked a sprained ankle) and went to an exhibit of pre-Industrial Age inventions at the Rockville Science Museum.

Oddly enough, there was only one bookshelf, darkened in shadows, as if to hide its secrets. Dusty tattered books that looked even older than those in the Rare Book Room spotted the shelves like a gap-toothed smile. The top shelf held no books at all—only a row of jars containing what looked like honey.

Miss DeHart gestured for the kids to have a seat in the chairs that surrounded a sprawling, dark oak table. "Please, sit down," she said with a courteous smile.

The librarians joined them, finding their seats quickly and without discussion, like a family gathering at the dinner table. Dr. Grunspan ran his fingers through the chaos of his hair and then tapped them on the cover of *The Dominion Glass*, which rested, re-bound, on the table before him. "Where to begin?" he said thoughtfully.

*How about the fact that all of you are fifth-degree black belts?*

Jay thought, looking back at the mentor he thought he had known. *Is kung fu now standard training in librarian school?*

Then, as if reading his mind, Dr. Grunspan continued, "We are not, as you might expect, simple librarians." He looked at the four young faces around the table, as if gauging their readiness for what he was about to tell them. "We belong to an organization called the Association for Paranormal Matters."

There was a long pause, and for a moment, deep in the library's basement, under the limestone roof, it was completely silent.

"I've never heard of it," Jay said finally. He wasn't sure what to believe. "Is—is it new?" he asked.

"It is very, very old," Dr. Grunspan replied. "*That* is why you've never heard of it."

"We're not the sort of organization that advertises," Professor Penfield added, his wrinkles glowing with soft lantern light like streaks of lava.

Dr. Grunspan drew a deep breath. "The Association is devoted to preserving and protecting paranormal secrets," and as he spoke, his explanation took on the air of a lecture. "It has a long, valiant history, dating back over a thousand years. Today, there are agents across the world—undercover in libraries, universities, museums, and other bastions of intellectual inquiry. Wherever paranormal artifacts exist, there are members of the APM protecting them."

Danni scratched her head. "So, wait, you're basically saying that there are a bunch of undercover nerds all over

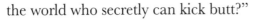 

the world who secretly can kick butt?"

"More or less," Dr. Grunspan answered.

"Brian, they're like the opposite of you," Danni said, amused.

Jay looked back at the bookcase that had swung open a moment ago. "So the Rare Book Room is full of paranormal secrets?"

"Many books are, yes, though not all. *The History of Doorknobs* has its limits in aiding matters paranormal." He winked at Danni. "Those books are the disguise—the distraction. But many of the books in the Rare Book Room, such as the one we hold here before us"—he gestured to *The Dominion Glass*—"are very powerful tomes, some full of paranormal wisdom, some magical in and of themselves. In the wrong hands, they can be very dangerous."

"What do you mean?" Jay asked brusquely—his curiosity was starting to override his manners. "Like who?"

"Those who would use them for their own less-than-noble purposes," Dr. Grunspan answered, not really answering at all.

"People like Pross?"

Dr. Grunspan's voice was grave and low. "We had no idea Pross was anything other than what his business card described—a part of the Global Digitization Initiative. We hired him because we needed these books digitized, lest something happen to them and all of the magic and knowledge within them be lost. As it is, we have lost a great many important books in the fire."

"Tragic," Professor Penfield echoed.

"Once the digitizing began, the guardian ghosts awoke," Dr. Grunspan said. "We thought they were just pests impeding our efforts to digitize the books, but now, of course, we realize…"

"They were protecting the books from Pross," Miss DeHart concluded.

"I hated the idea from the beginning," Professor Penfield grumbled, the expression on his face even crankier than usual.

"The professor felt that the digitized text would be vulnerable to theft," Dr. Grunspan said. "And, of course, his concern turned out to be regrettably prophetic."

"Of course," Pam said, nodding. She then turned to Jay and mouthed, "*What?*"

"But again," Dr. Grunspan said, "at the time, we were oblivious to Pross's agenda. We simply wanted the ghosts vanquished so we could complete the digitizing project."

"Why didn't you take on the ghosts?" Jay asked. "If you're part of this Association, why contact us?"

The librarians exchanged looks. Professor Penfield looked down and shook his well-groomed head.

"Two reasons," Dr. Grunspan said. "First, we did not want to—to use the colloquial—blow our cover. Until this point, as far as anyone in Rockville knew, we were just librarians whose most pressing concerns were retrieving overdue books and preserving old copies of *Highlights* magazine."

Brian glanced at Professor Penfield; his cane was nowhere to be seen. "So," Brian said, "you're not…"

"A doddering old coot?" Professor Penfield pushed his chair back from the table, stood up, straightened his bow tie, and launched into a perfect backflip. He landed squarely on his feet and promptly sat back in his chair. "You tell me."

Dr. Grunspan smiled. "Despite the measures we have taken to hide our true identities, Pross will share his newfound discoveries with his colleagues. They will conclude, correctly, that our shelves are stocked with scores of important paranormal books. And this makes our little library vulnerable."

Jay looked over Dr. Grunspan's shoulder at the books hiding in the half-light behind him. "What's the second reason you came to us?" Jay asked.

"We made a choice," Dr. Grunspan said, "to test you."

"You were testing us?!" Pam exclaimed. "We almost died!"

"We're sorry we put you in such danger," Miss DeHart said. "We never intended that."

Dr. Grunspan sighed. "As you can see from Pross's theft, there are times when we fall short. We are stretched thin and we grow old."

Professor Penfield harrumphed as Dr. Grunspan continued: "The truth is that we are actively searching for new members of the Association, and we have been monitoring your work—that much is true. Suffice it to say, we've been very impressed." The other librarians nodded in agreement.

"Talk about trial by fire," Danni said in disbelief.

Jay stammered, suddenly a little hurt, "So… all this time you were helping me… you… were *testing* me?"

Dr. Grunspan looked directly into Jay's eyes. "No, Jay. I have always been and still am intent on helping you achieve your personal goals. I just realized along the way that you and your friends were perfect candidates to be the next generation of the Association."

"So you never intended us to be in danger," Pam said. She pulled out the blank piece of paper. "But now, according to your letter, you seem okay to place us in…" Pam looked at the paper to quote it, but the writing had faded, so she had to use her memory as best as she could. "Uh… I believe it was 'great peril'…"

"We did not want to sugarcoat it," Miss DeHart said.

"Is it about that book?" Jay asked. "Is it important?"

"Yes," Dr. Grunspan said. "And yes."

"And we let him get it." Jay hung his head.

"Yes," Dr. Grunspan said. "And no."

Professor Penfield laughed. "Little snits like Pross don't understand something very important. To him, the newer the technology, the more powerful. But the truth is, when it comes to the paranormal, the opposite is true."

"Electromagnetic field detectors and ion generators are nice," Miss DeHart explained. "But there are older… *technologies*, for lack of a better word, that are far more useful to a paranormal investigator."

Dr. Grunspan rose from his chair and walked to the dark wooden bookshelf behind him. "Pross scanned the book and, having done so, he now has some important information that will help him on his quest for the Dominion Glass." He pulled out a thick brown book and blew the dust from its cover. "However, there are some things in books that cannot be digitized. Things that are lost in the process. Things that only the realness—the *thereness*—of paper can hold in its tiny threads."

"Books are magical," Professor Penfield added, and for the first time there was light in his voice. "They have souls in them, spirit to them. These things cannot be copied any more than a photo can copy your soul."

Dr. Grunspan handed the book to Jay. A design of coiling vines was etched into the cloth cover, giving the illusion of carved wood. Strangely, the book had no title. Jay flipped through its pages—they were all blank.

"Citric acid?"

Dr. Grunspan laughed. "No. This book holds within it something substantially more intriguing than a fruit juice."

He reached toward a small mahogany chest beside the bookcase and slid open the top drawer. It was full of assorted trinkets—things that gleamed and glistened in the lantern light—made of lustrous metals, glass, and gemstones. As Dr. Grunspan dipped his hand into the drawer, his thin, knobby fingers dancing over its contents, Jay was reminded of the claw-machine games at arcades.

Finally, Dr. Grunspan's bony hand clasped a pair of gold-rimmed spectacles and pulled them from the drawer. "Try these on," he said, handing the glasses to Jay.

The glasses were slightly too big for Jay's face, but they perched securely on the little bump on his nose. He wasn't sure what was supposed to be happening; everything looked exactly the same. They didn't even seem to have a prescription.

Through the rectangular lenses, Jay caught a slim smile curling on Dr. Grunspan's face. The others stared at him, waiting for him to speak, but there was nothing for him to say. Then he looked down at the blank book. It was no longer blank.

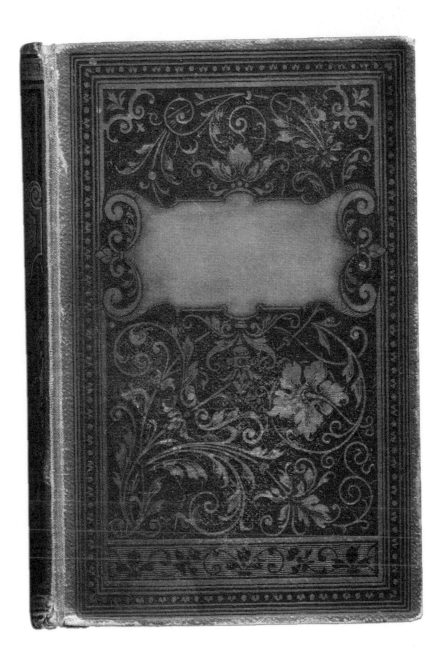

# CHAPTER NINE

## READING BEHIND THE LINES

"Whoa," Jay said, sliding his fingers over the book's cover.

"What is it?" Danni asked. "Do you see something?"

Next to Jay, Pam squinted at the book cover. In the pattern's swirls and curves, she thought she saw a few stray letters take shape. *That couldn't be right,* she thought, just as Jay read the title aloud: "*Paranormal Lore: An Incomplete Guide Assembled by Various Wraiths, Phantoms, Spectres, and Other Sundry Apparitions.*"

"Books are more interesting on the inside," Professor Penfield said. Then, after Jay didn't get the hint, he added crankily, "Open it."

Jay pulled open the cover: Pages that were blank a minute ago were suddenly full of illustrations and text scribbled in a medley of different handwritings. The strange writing glimmered like dewy spiderwebs in the moonlight.

"Ghostwriting," Dr. Grunspan said, smiling.

"Like someone secretly writing who isn't the author?" Danni asked.

"Like the author is a ghost."

"You can't digitize *that*," Professor Penfield announced with an air of triumph.

"The writing is invisible to the living," Dr. Grunspan added. "Unless, of course, they wear pneumaticles."

"Noo-mat-uh-what?" Pam asked.

"Noo-mat-uh-culls." Miss DeHart sounded out the word slowly, pronouncing each syllable as if speaking to preschoolers. She picked a pen from her shirt pocket—one of many that peeked over the pocket's lip—leaned over the table, and wrote the word on a page of the *Paranormal Lore* book. Only Jay noticed that she wrote right over a piece of ghostwriting that described how to remove a spirit possessing a mortal's body.

Miss DeHart neatly circled the first half of the word. "'Pneuma' is Greek for 'spirit.'" She then circled the middle of the word. "And 'mati' is Greek for—"

"Eye," Brian said.

"Very good," Miss DeHart said, looking up from the book. As her laserlike stare settled on him, Brian's cheeks flushed and he quickly looked away.

"Spirit eyes," Jay said, putting it together.

"Not surprisingly," Dr. Grunspan continued, "ghosts have the most insight into matters of the paranormal. Each spirit adds a bit of knowledge. They do this until a book is full—though, as the title says, nothing is ever complete. Or completely complete, at any rate."

"So it's like a Wikipedia for ghosts," Pam said.

"Wiccanpedia," Danni said brightly.

"In a sense," Miss DeHart laughed, stuffing the pen back into her pocket. "They write by thinking the words onto the page, but they all still have their own unique psychic handwriting."

"Understand that ghostwriting is not restricted to books such as this," Dr. Grunspan explained, pointing his bony finger at the page that Jay was reading (a debate between two spirits about whether it was possible to make just one part of the body invisible). "Ghosts often write in books written by mortals as well," he continued, "scribbling in the margins, correcting information, or elaborating on content with things only the dead can know."

Dr. Grunspan's words echoed in Pam's mind as he unlatched the four clasps of *The Dominion Glass*. "You all are probably curious about what exactly the fuss is about," he said, opening the cover.

"What is the Dominion Glass?" Jay asked. "I couldn't find it in the EP."

Dr. Grunspan pushed the open book toward Jay. "This will explain."

Jay started to take off the pneumaticles.

"No, no. Keep those on," Dr. Grunspan said. "You will find them useful. It appears that ghosts have had an easier time finding this book than we have."

Dear fellow APM member,

In this book are instructions to locate and uncover the Dominion Glass. I can only hope that your pursuit of the Glass stems from your desire to keep it safe, not to invoke its power.

Formed in the veins of Rockville's limestone caves thousands of years ago, the Dominion Glass is actually a small crystal shard made of rose quartz and topaz. Tales passed on from ghost to ghost tell of an ancient warlock who discovered the spiritual potential of the mineral and, through the blackest of dark magic, enchanted it.

The crystal was called the Dominion Glass because it is believed to allow the wielder of the artifact to summon and control spirits of the dead. The exact powers of the Glass are a matter of debate, and such is not the subject of this book, nor are the nature of the incantations to invoke those powers.

It is said that the Glass can be wielded only by mortals and will pass through the hand of a ghost. This is by design of its creator, who intended the crystal as a means of a mortal (presumably himself) having mastery over ghosts.

Since the earthquake of 1998, the Glass has been housed at the top of the Cliffs of Death, locked away in a crypt, protected by enchantments, and accessible only by a very special one-of-a-kind Key.

The directions to the Key are spelled out in this book. It is with this Key that you may claim the Dominion Glass.

—Ivan Warga, APM

Dr. Grunspan continued to speak, but Jay didn't hear a thing he said. He was transfixed by what he was reading: *"… spiritual potential… black magic… the power to summon… spirits of the dead…"*

When Jay finished reading—twice to himself, and once aloud—he took off the pneumaticles. "So with the glass, you can summon a specific spirit? Like someone in particular?" He tried to ask in a calm, professional way, but Dr. Grunspan eyed him peculiarly.

"Possibly," Miss DeHart said. "We aren't sure of its precise powers."

"What does it mean by 'controlling spirits'?" Danni asked. "Can you make the ghosts do your bidding—like zombies and Frankensteins and stuff?"

"It's hard to say," Miss DeHart said. "Beyond the first page, this book says very little about the actual powers of the glass."

"How many spirits can you summon?" Brian asked. "Can you have, like, a whole gang of ghosts or just—"

"We're researching the matter," Professor Penfield said gruffly, waving his arm as if swatting away bothersome flies.

Jay, however, wasn't concerned about zombies or Frankensteins or ghost gangs. He was thinking about just one ghost, and the chance, finally, to find him. "How do you use it?" he asked. And then, upon seeing the looks he got from both the librarians and his friends, he rephrased his question. "You know, how would someone like Pross activate the glass?"

"That," Dr. Grunspan said, "is thankfully not discussed in this book. And we hope we will never have to find out. Not everyone shares this opinion, however. If the wrong person were to obtain the artifact, it could be eminently problematic."

Both Pam and Danni turned to Brian for a translation.

"Bad," Brian mouthed silently, and while Danni correctly read his lips, Pam mistakenly thought he said "bed" and was completely confused.

"So the book contains directions to the key?" Jay asked.

Dr. Grunspan nodded. "Yes, and only with that key can you unlock the glass." He clasped his hands together, and as he spoke in the glow of the lanterns, Jay felt like they were all sitting around the campfire, sharing ghost stories—ghost stories that just happened to be completely and utterly real.

"Those who hid the key," Dr. Grunspan continued, "were members of the Association. They sought to make the key difficult to find, intending that only Association agents would be able to locate it. They brought the one copy of the book to our library for safekeeping." He looked down at the book solemnly. "We, of course, let Mr. Warga down."

Brian reached over and pulled the book toward him. Before reading a book, he always flipped through its pages. It was a speed-reading technique he had learned about, a way to give the brain a kind of head start before actually reading. "There are all kinds of weird poems and maps and stuff in here," he said as the pages fluttered before him in a jumble of letters and pictures.

"The map is not simply a straightforward, here-to-there map," Miss DeHart said. "For further protection, they filled it with puzzles and riddles. They didn't want anyone to be able to randomly stumble upon the course to find the key."

"Even so," Professor Penfield growled, "with a scan of the pages, it is still possible—though difficult—for someone outside the Association to find the Glass." He gritted his teeth. "Pross might be a little twit, but he's an intelligent little twit."

"I'm afraid that's true," Dr. Grunspan said, taking back the book from Brian. "However, as you saw with the pneumaticles, there are clues in the book that Pross's digital copy will not have. There will be more of them. And that will give you an advantage."

Pam nodded in agreement before fully realizing what he had just said. "Wait, what do you mean 'will give *you* an advantage'?" she asked, a bit of panic bubbling in her voice.

Dr. Grunspan looked at his colleagues. Professor Penfield leaned back, looked away, and threw his hands up in resignation.

"After much thought and"—he looked at Penfield again—"rigorous debate, we've decided we want you to use this book to hunt for the Dominion Glass."

Pam was shocked. "*Us?* As in *we?* Aren't you more

qualified for something like this? Black magic, ancient warlocks—that's kind of advanced stuff, isn't it?"

Dr. Grunspan turned to Pam. "Pross has undoubtedly informed his associates of the nature of our library and its keepers. Since our identities as agents have been revealed, we would likely be followed, potentially leading Pross right to the key."

"They won't expect you to go after the glass," Miss DeHart said. "Pross would never think we would send kids on something so…"

"Dangerous?" Pam offered with an expectant stare.

"Important," Miss DeHart said.

Dr. Grunspan continued to make his argument with the steady logic borne of a career in academics. "Furthermore," he said, "as I mentioned, since the library's identity has been compromised, the Rare Book Room is now extremely vulnerable. We need to immediately relocate the books. As important as *The Dominion Glass* is, there are even more precious books in this collection."

"There are?" Jay wondered aloud. "Are there other books about summoning ghosts?"

But Dr. Grunspan, yet again, did not give Jay the answer he was looking for. Instead, he narrowed his eyes and said, "It took some thought, but I have put together a plan. Miss DeHart and Professor Penfield will collect the most important books in our library and take them to a number of new, secure locations. You four will go for the key, unlock the glass, and bring it to us. Meanwhile, I will meet with senior members of the Association and pursue the leads on Pross's superior."

"Wait—so he's not doing this alone?" Jay beat Danni to the question.

"No," Dr. Grunspan said. "Our intelligence suggests Pross is working for someone."

"He's just a mercenary," Professor Penfield scowled, disdain crackling in his voice. "Probably just looking for a payday to buy more of his little gadgets."

Dr. Grunspan nodded. "If I can confirm for whom Pross is working, we can defuse the real threat. Then, even if Pross gets the glass, he will have no one to give it to." He leaned forward in his chair, and several strands of white hair collapsed over his face. "Consider this mission your true test," he said, "and your escapade in the Rare Book Room a mere warm-up quiz by comparison." His silver eyes gleamed and the wisps of his hair blanched like a sunlit waterfall. "Complete it successfully," he continued, "and we will officially welcome you into the ranks of the Association."

The ghost hunters did their best to choke down their surprise at what Dr. Grunspan had just proposed. Within the five seconds of silence that followed, they looked at one another in just about every possible combination, each hoping the other might give some hint about how to properly react.

"We cannot force you to do this, of course," Dr. Grunspan said, swiftly regaining their attention. "And I will not lie to you: Aside from the danger of Pross and his little toys, you are bound to confront other threats, both natural and paranormal."

Pam, Brian, and Danni let out a collective sigh.

"However," Dr. Grunspan continued, "if you truly want to be ghost hunters, I would encourage you to follow a cardinal rule of paranormal investigation." He turned to Jay. "Make the most of the moments that present themselves," he said, his voice growing wistful and smoky. "Moments are, in the end, all that we have."

It was something that Jay had heard Dr. Grunspan talk about before, although he never realized that he was speaking from a place of such experience and authority. For one thing, split-second decisions and quick action could make all the difference when battling ghosts—that was true. But what Dr. Grunspan seemed to be implying was that this was an incredible opportunity—a chance to become part of a remarkable organization steeped in centuries' worth of paranormal wisdom. And, of course, there was another opportunity unfolding with this mission as well, one that Jay chose not to talk about with Dr. Grunspan, or with anyone else for that matter.

"We'll do it," Jay replied.

The others looked at him in disbelief.

Miss DeHart flashed her perfect teeth in a smile. "I suppose we should get you geared up then."

# CHAPTER TEN

## OUT WITH THE NEW, IN WITH THE OLD

D r. Grunspan told Jay that he could keep the pneumaticles, and he quickly browsed through the ghostwritten pages of the *Paranormal Lore* book. He realized that along with their own distinct handwriting, the ghosts all had individual personalities and writing styles.

Older ghosts wrote more formally, while those who died recently were sparing in their words and much more casual with their language. Jay continued his talent for guessing ghosts' death dates. He pegged one ghost as having died in the early 1970s because he described the spirit world as "groovy" and "far out." The ghost even used the phrase "Right on!" to agree with a previous ghost's comment. Another ghost was a former English teacher who delighted in proofreading and correcting other spirits' grammatical mistakes.

As Jay skimmed the books, he noticed Pam looking over his shoulder.

"What?" he asked. "Do you want to look?"

Before Pam could answer, Miss DeHart called out, "I trust you know how to use this, Pam."

With a heavy thud, she placed a crystal ball on the table. The glossy orb, about the size of a softball, sat on a small wooden stand. It was made of glass, but it was so full of dense gray fog that it looked more like stainless steel.

Pam looked into the ball and saw her distorted reflection staring back at her. "My mom thinks I'm not ready."

"Then you'll need to practice," Miss DeHart replied cheerfully.

Pam placed her hands at the base of the ball, stared into it—really tried to *gaze*—and strained to summon a vision of the future.

Miss DeHart didn't need to be psychic to sense Pam's frustration. "Don't fret," she said. "The way Professor Penfield tells it, when your mom was your age, she couldn't even predict what color M&M she was going to pull from the bag."

"It's true," Professor Penfield chuckled. "I distinctly remember she just kept saying, 'Green, green, green,' thinking eventually she'd have to get it right."

"You know my mom?" Pam asked eagerly, looking up from the crystal ball.

"She was a student of mine once," he answered. He shook his head. "Showed very little promise, that one."

Pam's eyes brightened under her bangs as Professor Penfield hunched over and picked up what looked like a cross between an old camera and a DustBuster. Black metal plates covered the camera's body, while a metal snout stretched to an oval lens at its mouth. Connected to the device by a coiled wire was a half-inch-thick transparent plate. Like the crystal ball, the plate was made of glass, but this glass was old and uneven, full of rivulets and bubbles, framed in a worn-down border of black paint.

"Is that for orbs?" Danni asked the professor.

"No, digital cameras pick up orbs," he said. "This is a Kirlian camera. Do you know what that is?"

"It takes pictures of auras," Danni replied eagerly.

"Go to the head of the class, young lady."

As Danni smiled, Professor Penfield aimed the camera at her and pressed a button.

"An aura represents a person's energy," he explained. "Very few people can see them, but the camera—which is over two hundred years old, by the way—can pick them up." He lifted the plate into the glow of the lantern light. "How do you know about Kirlian photography?" he asked Danni as colorful images bloomed on the glass.

"There's this M. T. Boesch story," Danni said, and she began to speak very fast. "It's about a fashion photographer who finds a Kirlian camera, and he starts taking pictures of all the famous supermodels. So, like, the public becomes totally fascinated with the auras. But the models' auras are plain because of their boring personalities, or even ugly because they're all bitter, jealous, and shallow and stuff. So eventually all the famous models are out of work, and people with colorful, warm auras—ugly or average-looking people with great personalities—become the models. And they're the ones giving autographs and being stalked by the paparazzi, who all now have Kirlian cameras. They even have inner-beauty pageants and everything. Anyway, so eventually the fame goes to the new models' heads, and their auras start reflecting their new shallow, arrogant, ugly sides, so they're all out of work too. In the end, the photographer decides to take pictures only of children."

"Ah, M. T. Boesch—my favorite author," Professor Penfield said, watching the shapes ooze, amoebalike, over the plate.

"Mine too!" Danni said excitedly.

Professor Penfield squinted at the glass and smiled, satisfied. "Heck of an aura you got there, Danni." He handed her the plate. A silhouette of her body was surrounded by a halo of deep purples, pinks, and greens, all radiating in wild, ever-changing patterns. "Those colors reveal a person of deep compassion and thoughtfulness," he told her as the blobs continued to shift and flow like spilled paint.

"Didn't you say that a book's spirit couldn't be digitized any more than a photo can copy your soul?" she asked.

"Nobody likes a smarty-pants, Danni," Professor Penfield snarled. "Except me." The professor hacked a deep laugh and patted Danni on her shoulder, which still stung from the ghost's chilling grip two days earlier.

"Brian, I have something for you as well," Dr. Grunspan

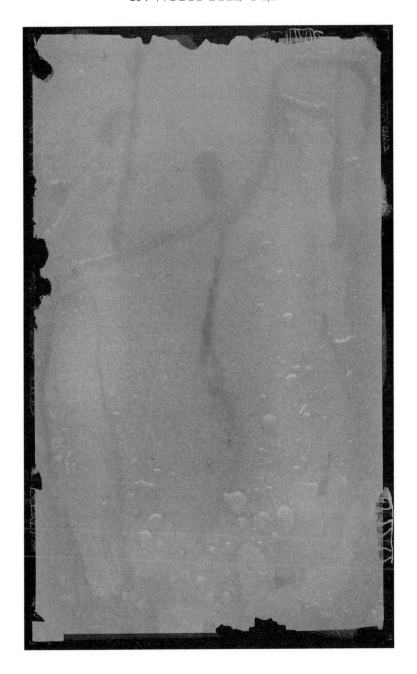

said, reaching into the drawer. "It's a gift that suits your prodigious perspicacity."

Brian hunched forward on his seat, a gleam of excitement in his eyes. "Ah, here it is," Dr. Grunspan said with a reverent tone. He turned back around and handed Brian a gray knit cap.

"A *hat?*" Brian asked, unable to hide both his surprise and disappointment.

"You'll want to keep warm," Dr. Grunspan replied matter-of-factly.

Brian turned the hat in his hands. "Um, thanks."

Mr. Grunspan smiled wryly. "That *hat* is woven from a rare metal alloy called sarinium. It takes the energy of the sun and transmits it into your scalp and through your skull, setting off an electromagnetic reaction in the synapses of your hypothalamus."

Jay could tell by the look on his face that even Brian was unable to follow Dr. Grunspan's explanation.

"It's a brain warmer," Dr. Grunspan said.

"Isn't that just another name for a hat?" Pam asked.

"Quite the contrary," Dr. Grunspan said. "Have you ever noticed that your best ideas often come to you during a long, hot shower or while basking on a sun-drenched beach? When the brain heats up, it functions more efficiently. This is the same idea, though the chemistry and physics are much more complicated."

"That sounds like new technology." Brian flipped the hat inside out, and it seemed to draw in the light from around him. "I thought you said old technology is more powerful."

Dr. Grunspan nodded. "There is a branch of paranormal science devoted to uniting the old ways with new technology. The metals in the hat are mined from a quarry charged with a unique paranormal energy. It's a very difficult discipline, this weaving together of magic and technological innovation, and only a few gifted minds can produce working devices. But when done right, the blend of old and new can be extremely potent."

"Bah," Professor Penfield groaned. "I'll stick with a divining rod any day."

Dr. Grunspan smiled and turned back to the bookcase. "One last thing," he said.

He reached to the top shelf, toward the row of short glass jars full of amber liquid. He brought one of the jars to the table, clasping it carefully and respectfully with both hands, as if holding a baby, before placing it on the table. The jar's golden liquid glowed in the light—it was thick, like maple syrup, and suspended in the middle was a slimy, curled tube.

"Gnarly," Danni said, bending down to look into the jar.

"Go ahead, open it up," Dr. Grunspan urged.

Danni obliged, eagerly unscrewing the lid. In an instant, her face contorted with disgust, and a half second later, so did the faces of her friends. "What is it?" she asked, clamping the lid back on the jar.

"Iguana intestine," Dr. Grunspan offered, calmly

tightening the lid. "The smell attracts nearby ghosts." He slid the jar toward Jay. "It's for you."

"Lucky you, Jay," Brian said, wiping away the lingering stench.

Jay picked up the jar. It felt surprisingly hot. His fingers tingled as the thick, syrupy liquid seeped around the soft, pale coil.

"Wait, it *attracts* ghosts?" Pam asked. "Why would you possibly want to *attract* ghosts?"

"You'd be surprised," Dr. Grunspan said, looking over at Jay.

Jay glanced back at him and then down at the glass jar, but his mind was somewhere else. He was back in the forest. Six years ago. He could feel the crisp, crumbling leaves beneath his feet. Gold light sliced through the treetops. *If he had just a moment longer… If he could have gotten closer to the ghost…* And then, as on that day, the vision of his father was lost as he heard Dr. Grunspan say, "Sometimes, the most useful tools are the least obvious."

Jay looked up from the jar to find that Dr. Grunspan was still looking at him. His unwavering stare made Jay feel uneasy. It was like a psychic's gaze into a crystal ball, as if Dr. Grunspan could see through him, into him—as if he could see his thoughts.

"Why do ghosts like lizard intestines?" Brian asked.

"Ghosts are attracted to energy," Dr. Grunspan answered. "They need energy to exist. That's why, of course, they create cold spots—as Jay explained to us so articulately outside the Rare Book Room." Dr. Grunspan held the jar aloft. "And of all the parts of a living being, it is one's center that is most spiritually charged—it is not the brain or the heart, but rather the middle of us that is deepest and most eternal."

"You can feel it," Miss DeHart said. "When you dig deep or feel something in your core, you're drawing on this energy."

"It's the reason we say, 'Go with your gut,'" Professor Penfield said.

"Or speak of a person 'having guts' when he is most courageous and true," Dr. Grunspan added. He turned back to the shelf behind him and looked up to the row of jars. "Human intestines, though more potent, would be, of course, impractical to cultivate. So we use lizards— creatures of surprisingly strong spiritual force."

"And smell," Professor Penfield added.

A gong sounded, echoing off the ridges of the limestone roof. Jay turned and saw that the sound was coming from a very unusual grandfather clock. Where there would normally be a clock face there was instead a series of hourglasses, all tilted at different angles, one spilling sand into the next. Jay had no idea how you were supposed to tell time from the arrangement, but the librarians eyed the clock with the same immediate understanding as someone checking their wristwatch.

"You all should be going," Dr. Grunspan said as the clock continued to chime. He buckled the four latches on

*The Dominion Glass* and handed it to Jay. "Pross has already started to endeavor for the key, and we must all begin the tasks before us."

The other librarians stood from the table, and the ghost hunters followed their lead, stuffing their new gifts into their backpacks as if packing away their books at the final school bell. Professor Penfield jabbed a button on the wall, and the bookshelf swung open.

"The success of this mission—as with most matters of the Association—hinges largely on your ability to keep it secret," Dr. Grunspan said as they made their way toward the open shelf.

"Do not use phones or e-mail to communicate about this—not with each other and not with us," Professor Penfield ordered sternly. "They can be traced."

"How will we get in touch with you?" Jay asked as he backed into the light spilling in from the Rare Book Room.

"We will get in touch with you about when and where to return the glass," Dr. Grunspan said. "As we have before."

"When will you be back?" Jay said.

"I cannot say. But the library is no longer a safe place. Do not return here unless we instruct you to do so." Dr. Grunspan stopped in the doorway. "There is an emergency exit at the end of the Reference section. As you leave, make sure you are not being followed. Find a secure place to review the book and begin the quest. Time," he said, looking back at the strange clock, "is slipping away."

# OUT WITH THE NEW,
# IN WITH THE OLD

"Be brave," Miss DeHart said as they stepped out into the Rare Book Room.

"But not stupid," Professor Penfield added.

"We are counting on you," Dr. Grunspan said seriously, and he fell from light to darkness as the bookshelf began to close.

"We won't let you down," Jay said. "I promise." And the bookshelf swiveled shut.

# CHAPTER ELEVEN

## A GRAVE CHALLENGE

"I still can't believe you just immediately agreed to it, Jay," Pam said as they settled into their seats around the spirit board kitchen table. "I mean, normally at least we discuss these sorts of things before we go skipping into unknown danger."

"This is the chance of a lifetime," Jay said, scooting his chair up to the board's crescent moon. "Think about how much we'll learn when we become part of the Association."

"If we survive."

"It was just a Taser."

"*Just a Taser!?*" Pam swiped her bangs from her face so Jay could see how serious she was. "Right. Just fifty thousand volts coursing through your veins. Do you know how much that is, Jay?"

"A lot?"

"Put it this way: For the rest of your life, you'd be turning your jelly sandwiches to toast as soon as you bit into them."

Jay shrugged. "Sounds kind of cool to me."

He smiled playfully at Pam, who eventually smiled herself and shook her head. "You're insane."

Danni walked her fingers across the spirit board table, absentmindedly tracing letters. "Who do you think Pross is working for? It seems to be a big deal."

"I don't know," Jay said, spinning the planchette. "Dr. Grunspan just said he was pursuing some leads."

"Ask the board, Pam," Brian said. He was thumbing through *The Dominion Glass,* and his eyes began to dance around the puzzles he was finding inside.

"Good idea," Jay agreed, sliding the planchette over to Pam like it was a paper football.

"Come on," she moped. "Are you seriously going to make me do this?"

"I don't see Momma or Darla here," Jay said. "Where are they anyway?"

"With Dad at the police station," Pam said glumly. "To help him with some psychometry."

"Psychometry?" Brian said, looking up from the book. "What's that?"

"Wow, Brian doesn't know a word, and I do," Pam taunted. *"I'm not telling...,"* Pam sang mockingly.

"It's on all the crime shows," Danni said, ruining Pam's fun. "It's when you pick up an object and you can see in your mind who's touched it."

"Yeah, and if you're really good," Pam added, "you can see the object's whole history. The police give Dad murder weapons and stuff."

"Cool," Danni said. "So can he, like, see all the crimes as if they're happening?"

"I don't know. Dad doesn't share the details. Anyway, he's psychically stumped and he called Momma and Darla in to help him."

"But not you?" Brian teased.

"Shut up," Pam snapped.

"Here's your chance to prove them wrong," Jay said, tapping the table invitingly.

Pam sighed. "Fine, whatever." She steadied the planchette on the board, closed her eyes, and took a deep, soulful breath. This time when she spoke, she sounded like her sister—or, more accurately, like a bad impression of her—as artificially deep as the voice Brian used to impress Miss DeHart. "Spirits of the Great Beyond…," she rumbled. "Guide my hand… Fill me with your energy and tell me… Who wants the Dominion Glass so bad?" The planchette slid over a letter. Then another. Then another.

"Your name again?" Brian said. "Unbelievable." He shook his head and then buried it again in the book.

"Maybe you should ask the crystal ball instead?" Jay suggested.

Pam was immediately defensive. "You can't ask specific questions to a crystal ball. You can just look at it and maybe, if you're lucky, a vague image of the future will appear." She shrugged. "We might as well all try. It's not like I have the gift any more than you guys do."

Each of them took a turn peering into the ball, and

though all of them did in fact see something, each was hesitant to share what it was they had seen.

When they finally revealed their respective visions, a simmering panic ensued.

"Maybe it's a good thing?" Danni said in an effort to brighten the mood.

"*A good thing?*" Brian exclaimed. "Please explain to me how exactly visions of a skull, a sword, and a gravestone are a *good thing?*"

"I don't know," she shrugged. "Like, maybe someone

will give us a sword… which we'll sell for a fortune to a friendly skeleton… who then returns happily to his unmarked grave."

"What about the symbol?" Brian pressed.

"Maybe it's a symbol of good luck," Danni said.

"Let's try again." Jay picked up the crystal ball and started shaking it madly.

Pam grabbed Jay's hand. "Stop it! It's not some novelty Magic 8 Ball!" She placed the ball delicately back on its stand. "And you can't keep looking into a crystal ball. It will weaken its power."

"Fine," Jay said. "Let's just look at the book then."

To Brian's delight, this wasn't going to be easy. Page one had already stumped them. The book began with a poem:

> *Eight brothers from one mother*
> *Lie beside one another*
> *Sleeping gently by their mum*
> *Quiet as the morning sun*
> *Crossing gently 'bout the stones*
> *Keep your steps as straight as bones*
> *Know that you can use just four*
> *Straight lines to walk, and not one more.*
> *In the end, the course you'll find*
> *If you link the dark stones nine*

"So, what? We need to find eight babies?" Pam asked. "Like on that show *Kate Plus Eight?*"

Brian shook his head dismissively. "This book was written more than ten years ago, when they hid the key. If it was describing babies, they'd be older by now."

"Crossing stones?" Jay said. "Maybe we have to cross a river or something."

Brian looked at the riddle and began scratching his eyebrow. "'Morning sun.' That's an interesting choice of words." The pace of his eyebrow-scratching quickened. "Both 'morning' and 'sun' have homophones," he pointed out to an audience of blank stares. "Words that sound the same but are spelled differently," he clarified.

Brian wrote down the phrase "mourning son" so everyone could see.

Jay immediately understood. "The Tomb of the Eight Brothers," he said confidently. "That's what the stones are: their graves."

"What's the Tomb of the Eight Brothers?" Brian asked, jotting a checkmark on his paper as if giving himself a good grade.

Though Brian was the one with the near-photographic memory, when it came to the sick and sordid, Danni was a walking encyclopedia. The words tumbled out of her mouth as she gleefully unleashed an account of the horrid tale: "Two hundred years ago, a woman named Eileen Sinderson gave birth to eight sons. She was worth a fortune—like, megamillions—and each of her sons tried to prove that he loved her most so that someday she'd leave him all her money. They spent their whole lives faking their love for their mom, hoping they'd be chosen as the sole heir."

"I remember this," Pam said, looking down into the crystal ball as if trying to muster some hazy distant memory. "I read about it somewhere. They ended up all fighting or something."

Danni nodded, and her voice was light and playful as she described the story's gruesome ending. "When Eileen died, she had no will, so each of the sons claimed that her fortune was his. They fought over it and all ended up killing each other in a violent bloodbath."

"And the tomb?" Brian asked.

"The brothers all asked to be buried near their mother. Supposedly she was buried with some of her money."

"I guess they thought what they couldn't get in life, they could get in death," Pam said curiously.

"Guess so," Danni said. Then, in a spooky voice, she added, "They say you can still hear the clanging of weapons as their spirits battle under the ground."

"Only one way to find out," Jay said. And he headed for the door.

Cemeteries, Jay had always thought, were peaceful places during the day. The grass was neatly maintained. The lawns were wide and open and well landscaped. Everyone was polite and spoke in hushed tones. They were basically golf courses, but with big stone slabs in the fairways.

And since it was daytime, there was nothing to be afraid

of. Even ghost-hunting novices knew that in cemeteries, ghosts only came out at night. There were different theories as to why. One claimed it was out of respect for the living, to let them remember and mourn their loved ones in peace.

Jay had actually spoken to several ghosts about their resting places, and they all told Jay the same thing: Cemeteries were designed and constructed for the living, not for the dead. They told Jay that ghosts didn't care if they had a stone on top of their graves any more than a living person would want a stone on top of her bunk bed. But having a place to come remember and mourn served a purpose: It gave comfort to those who had lost a loved one. Jay was made starkly aware of this purpose by feeling its absence. He had had no grave to come to, no quiet place to mourn the loss of his father; no body, no coffin, no gravesite—just the pictures on his nightstand.

There was another theory about why ghosts only emerged at night. It held that spirits were busy haunting other sites during the day, around places or people to which they were tethered, and that they simply returned to the cemetery at sundown. In other words, they had day jobs. One thing ghost hunters did agree on was that at night, cemeteries were a different story. They became graveyards and were then the property of the dead. And while some graveyard ghosts might be peaceful, others might not, and few ghost hunters thought it wise to hang around to figure out which were which.

At the moment, all was well. The sun shined brightly on Oak Gardens Memorial Cemetery, and Jay led the way down a gravel path that wove through the grounds. On either side of the path were the gravesites, some marked with simple plaques, others with ornate stones—all in all, pleasant enough surroundings.

Pam rattled off the names she saw on the stones: "McAullife… Smith… Kesselman… How are we supposed to find them? It's not like they're in alphabetical order."

"Or chronological order," Brian said, scanning the graves on his left.

"There," Danni said, pointing ahead and hurrying over to a private corner of the cemetery.

Nine flat, marbled gravestones were arranged in a three-by-three grid. On each of the eight outer stones was the name of one of the eight brothers. The center stone was engraved with just three letters.

"'Wow,'" Danni said, reading from the center stone. She circled to the other side. 'Oh, no, 'Mom.'"

"It's like a tic-tac-toe board of graves," Pam said. "Do we have to play tic-tac-toe?"

"Yeah," Brian mocked. "We have to play tic-tac-toe against a ghost. That would be a brilliant challenge—we'd just end up tying over and over." He walked the perimeter of the graves, noting the names and dates on the stones. "Read the second part of the poem again," he said to Jay.

Jay unlatched the clasps, opened the book and read aloud: "Crossing gently 'bout the stones… Keep your steps as straight as bones… Know that you can use just four… Straight lines to walk, and not one more… In the end, the course you'll find… If you link the dark stones nine."

Pam went white. "It wants us to walk on their graves. Seems a bit disrespectful." Her eyes wandered over the graves. "Not to mention creepy."

"Well, somebody's been walking these graves recently," Danni said, pointing to a footprint in the sunbaked ground between brothers Charles and Leopold. She removed some biofoam and pressed it onto a print. "Hmm," she muttered thoughtfully, crawling on the ground from grave to grave like she was looking for a lost contact lens. "I think someone walked from Marcus to Leopold." She placed the foam into a second print. "Then maybe down to Wallace? It's tough to tell. The grass isn't great for prints. Maybe—"

"Did you guys hear that?" Pam jerked her head back toward the path.

"What?" Jay asked, clasping the book closed.

"I thought I heard something." After a few minutes, when nothing appeared, Pam chalked the noise up to her "fertile imagination." Or was something going on beneath her? She shuddered at the thought.

Brian crouched down and scanned the graves. He mumbled to himself, "Cross gently about the stones… Keep your steps as straight as bones… Know that you cannot use more… Straight lines to walk than just four." His pinkie raced against his eyebrow and he bit his lip in concentration. "We have to connect all the stones by

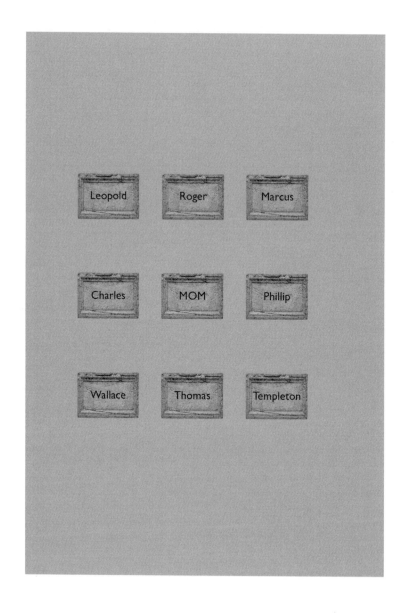

walking in four consecutive straight lines," he said. "It's a puzzle."

"You sure?" Pam asked.

"I've seen stuff sort of like this before. Usually it's connecting dots with a pencil, though." He stepped toward brother Marcus's gravestone and then stopped.

"What's the matter?" Jay asked him.

Brian looked down at his feet. "I just feel like an arm is going to reach out from the ground or something." He moved gingerly, as if he was stepping onto a frozen pond, unsure if the ice was thick enough to hold. After a few tiptoed steps, confident that nothing was going to burst through the soil and grab his ankle, he continued walking in a straight line. "Shouldn't be too hard," he said as he pivoted away from brother Templeton's grave.

Brian was wrong. He was used to being wrong on purpose in school, but here he was genuinely stumped, as were the rest of his secret friends. For hours they tried to fulfill the poem's requirements: *Connect all nine stones with four consecutive straight lines.*

By the end of the day, all they had managed to do was wear down the grass between the graves, making them look like baseball bases connected by a dirt infield.

"We've mucked up the footprints," Danni said. There was a rare irritated tone to her voice.

"So what?" Brian said, frustrated.

"They might have been a clue," she said, exasperated.

Exhausted both mentally and physically, Pam sat down,

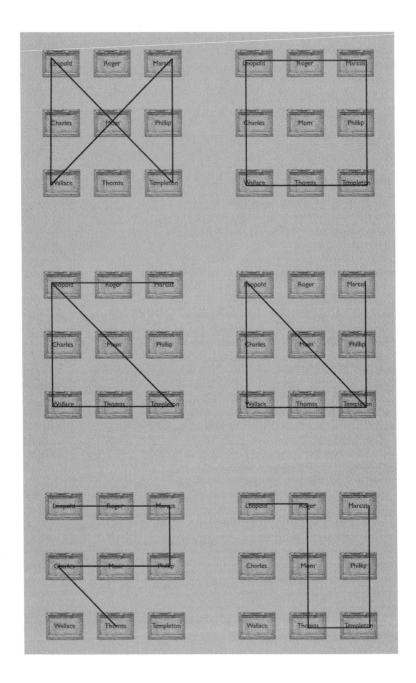

right on brother Roger. "This is pointless," she said. "We're going in circles, or squares, or triangles, or whatever." She looked at the horizon, bruising pink to purple. The graves' shadows grew long, darkening the gravesites. "I'm gonna sleep on this one. Maybe I'll get a vision in a dream."

"Right," Brian snapped. "Like your name again?"

"Don't take it out on me just because you can't solve a stupid puzzle," she shot back.

Brian said nothing. He just kept walking.

"I'll see if I can figure out anything about these footprints," Danni said.

"I'll check my books," Jay added, thinking Brian would get the hint that it was time to stop. But he kept on going, mumbling to himself as he raced from grave to grave. "It's getting dark, Brian," Jay told him. "Don't stick around too much longer."

Though he didn't say anything, Brian was kind of glad his friends were leaving. He did his best thinking alone, in silence and solitude, just a puzzle and his brain pitted against each other—two friendly adversaries, each with a healthy respect for its opponent. But it wasn't always this way.

When Brian was in first grade, his family moved to Rockville. At the time, he was going through what could generously be called an awkward stage. He was short, pudgy, and had thick, dark-rimmed glasses, not unlike those Mr. Linkins wore.

On his first day of school, the teacher, Mrs. Reese, was

reciting the names of the planets. "Mercury, Venus, Earth, Mars, Jupiter, Saturn, Uranus, Neptune, and, of course, Pluto," she said, seeming very pleased with herself.

Brian raised his hand. "Actually, Pluto isn't technically a planet. It was recently reclassified as a dwarf planet."

Mrs. Reese stared at him—she looked shocked—and the class was silent for a moment.

"What a dork!" Amid the tsunami of student laughter, Brian turned to see a tall blond kid glaring at him.

Randy Mingo looked as tough as a six-year-old possibly could. He had a cruel smile, scrapes all over his elbows and knees, and sand-colored hair that was parted in the middle, swept up like miniature McDonald's arches. Brian quickly turned the other way. A few seats away, Beth Jaffe, the prettiest girl in school, stifled a giggle as she leaned over to another girl and whispered. Brian never forgot what he heard her say: "Look at his glasses. He looks like a giant bug."

"Settle down," Mrs. Reese said before explaining, incorrectly, that Saturn was the only planet with rings.

Humiliated beyond recovery, Brian asked his parents to switch him to a new school. Before he stepped into the halls of Rockville Elementary, he took off his glasses, sucked in his gut, and the charade of stupidity began. He stammered during his reading evaluation to make sure to get into the lowest reading group. He claimed that Pluto was indeed a planet, as was the sun, the moon, and Krypton. He was quickly deemed stupid and, accordingly, was both respected by boys and admired by girls. The only subject where Brian applied himself was phys ed, and after a while, he became slim and fit, and, eventually, the best athlete in the school.

Brian still did puzzles and read with a reckless appetite, but it was always at home or hidden away somewhere, and nobody would have been the wiser if Jay hadn't come in after school one day to use Mr. Linkins's lab, only to find Brian huddled behind the coatrack reading a book on quantum physics. Jay made a deal with Brian to keep his secret intelligence under wraps if he would help with his ghost hunting. Brian agreed and soon became excited by the intellectual stimulation the paranormal world had to offer.

"I knew you were smart," Danni told Brian when he joined the team. "You always pause before answering wrong, like you're changing your answer. And when you misspell words, the wrong letters are written differently, like you're straining to write them."

"I knew too," Pam said.

"How?" Brian asked.

"Call it a hunch."

Five years later, Brian was using his brain the only way he knew how: in secret. He applied the same laser-like focus he used when solving Sudokus to the challenge before him. But as dusk threatened to turn into night, Brian continued to walk back and forth from stone to stone to no avail. Every once in a while, he thought he heard something scuttling in the twilight.

In the library, Professor Penfield checked the time on his cell phone; it read 12:37. Unable to set the time correctly on his phone, he had memorized that his clock was always 7 hours and 23 minutes slow, which meant it was now 8 p.m., closing time. He put on his matching charcoal overcoat and prepared to leave. "Do you really think it is wise to leave this quest to children?" he asked Dr. Grunspan.

"I know Jay. He can handle this."

Professor Penfield grumbled.

"You need to have faith in them, Rudolph," Dr. Grunspan said.

Professor Penfield nodded solemnly. "We'll find out soon enough."

The professor walked out the door toward the truck parked in the library's fire lane. Miss DeHart was wheeling the last cart of books into the truck's cabin.

"Let us know what you find out," Professor Penfield said, looking back at Dr. Grunspan.

"Of course."

"Good luck."

"And the very best to you." As the door shut, Dr. Grunspan sat down at a table and opened a book, as he did at the end of every day of his life. Another drop in an ocean of knowledge.

# CHAPTER TWELVE

## A SILENT VISITOR

That night it was Jay, not Pam, who had the vivid dreams.

Dr. Grunspan and Professor Penfield were in the library's secret room, debating something having to do with a humongous hourglass, nearly seven feet tall. Red, luminous crystals as large as marbles rattled through the glass's neck. Beside it, Jay noticed a chair made entirely of bones. He felt drawn to the chair and sat, resting his elbows on its skeletal arms.

In the darkness, eyes appeared, and, like a cat emerging from the shadows, Miss DeHart stepped toward him. "You're ready," she said. Jay's thoughts tumbled, emptying like the crystals in the hourglass. The chair became softer... softer... then he was in water.

His surroundings changed. Suddenly, he was back at the water park, only he was twelve, not six. Everything was going backward, like the world was being rewound. He was hoisted from the pool onto the bottom of the waterslide, droplets collecting from the air into a smooth, unbroken surface. He meandered up the slide over an upward trickle of water, until he slammed into a pair of arms. When he turned around, he saw his father smiling down at him, the bright sun beaming in the sky above. Michael Winnick faded into the sunlight—was lost in it—then was gone.

When Jay woke up, he instinctively began his morning routine. But as he reached over to his nightstand to grab the latest *Ghost Hunters Weekly*, his hand fell instead on *The Dominion Glass*. There was something on top of it.

He wiped the last drops of his dreams from his eyes and peered over at the nightstand, where he saw the pneumaticles resting tidily atop the book. That's not where he'd left them. He was sure he'd put them in his nightstand drawer. His first thought was that maybe he had sleepwalked, but he dismissed it right away. He often tossed and turned with adventurous dreams, but if he had ever walked in his sleep, his mom would have called nine doctors by now, padded the walls of the room, and, at the very least, devised some sort of bed harness to keep him "safe."

Someone or something had moved the pneumaticles. In fact, not only were the glasses on top of Warga's book, but the book was open to the "Tomb of the Eight Brothers" poem. Jay distinctly remembered closing the book before he went to sleep.

With wobbly, waking legs, he stood up, looked around the room, and crossed slowly to his closet. He felt ridiculous—like a four-year-old looking for the bogeyman. He took a deep breath, pulled the closet door open, and... nothing. He kept himself—with some effort—from checking under his bed. Instead, he walked back to the nightstand, picked up the pneumaticles, and put them on.

There was something written in the book—something that wasn't there before. He took the glasses off and the writing disappeared. Ghostwriting. How? Had he slept right through a haunting?

The next morning was a Saturday, so Jay met the gang at the tomb site very early. He told his mom he was going fishing, and though she feared fishhook wounds and snapping turtles, and gave Jay the typical "Be careful!" speech, it was a lot more bearable than the discussion that would have ensued if he had casually mentioned he was marching around a possibly cursed cemetery lot.

He wasted no time in relaying the mysterious message scrawled in the book. As always, everyone had a theory on how it got there.

"Maybe it was the ghost of one of the brothers," Pam suggested.

"What if it wasn't a ghost?" Danni asked as she dusted the book for fingerprints.

"But it's *ghostwriting!*" Pam replied.

Danni blew the fluorescent powder off the paper, and it sprinkled down like fairy dust onto brother Phillip's gravestone. "Well, I don't see any new prints other than Jay's," she said. (She had learned to recognize each of her

Eight brothers from one mother

Lie beside one another

Sleeping gently by their mum

Quiet as the morning sun

Crossing gently 'bout the stones

Keep your steps as straight as bones

Know that you can use just four

Straight lines to walk, and not one more

In the end, the course you'll find

If you link the dark stones nine

friends' prints by eye after making them repeatedly help her practice her crime-scene investigations.)

"Still," Brian said thoughtfully, "what if someone like Pross learned how to do it? Maybe he used some gadget or something."

"No," Jay said dismissively. "I don't think you can fake ghostwriting. And if it was someone living, I'm sure I would have woken up. I'm a light sleeper."

For almost an hour, they discussed what the ghostwriting might mean.

"Maybe 'think outside the box' means to think outside the coffin," Pam said. "A coffin is a box. Sort of."

Brian scoffed at her. "As opposed to thinking *inside* the coffin?"

"Ooh, do you think we have to dig them up?" Danni said excitedly.

"I think we should hold off on the grave robbing for now," Jay replied. He turned to Brian, nudged his head toward his backpack, and said, "Why don't you put your thinking cap on."

"Dude, I'm trying," Brian replied, annoyed. "Cut me some slack."

"No, I mean, use your brain-heater thing."

"Seriously?" Brian laughed. "You don't think that will actually work, do you?"

"Can't hurt."

Brian sighed, reached into his backpack, and pulled

out the hat. He looked around to make sure no one was around. "Happy?" he said to Jay, pulling it over his ears.

"Looks sharp." Jay cracked a smile as Brian walked away to think.

For the next few minutes, everyone kept quiet. Every so often, one of the others glanced over at Brian. Annoyed, he turned away from them and began fidgeting with the cap. Then he began pacing. "Think outside the box," he muttered to himself. Then more pacing... and stopping... and fidgeting with his hat... and staring off... and scratching his eyebrow.

He turned around. He stared off into the distance. He crouched low and looked at the ground as if reading a putting green, which inevitably made Jay think again about a golf course. All of a sudden, Brian stood up and seemed to be following something with his eyes. He hurried past the graves, then turned, and his eyes drifted across the graveyard.

"Is he seeing things now?" Pam asked Jay under her breath.

"I got it!" Brian announced.

"You got what?" Jay asked.

"The answer. The box is the square around the graves, the grid. We kept thinking you have to stop when you get to a gravestone and start a new line. But you need to keep walking."

Brian demonstrated the solution to the puzzle.

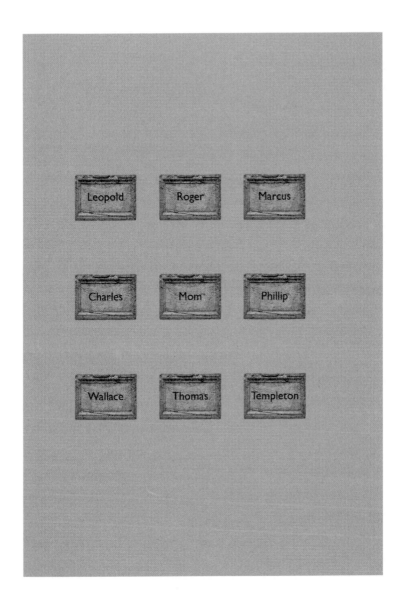

"Think outside the box," he said to himself with ten times the satisfaction he felt after scoring a winning soccer goal. "Jay, your ghostwriter just helped us big-time."

Jay looked down at the book. Whoever was haunting his house just gave them a hint. *What kind of ghost does that? And why?*

Before he had time to give any more thought to the matter, Pam blurted out, "Now what?" She looked around the cemetery—it was deserted. "Nothing's happening."

Brian recited the poem's final lines from memory. "In the end, the course you'll find… If you link the dark stones nine." A second after he finished the poem, he snapped his fingers. "I got it!" he said. "The path makes an arrow." He walked the pattern again, this time faster.

"Huh?" Danni said, watching Brian bustle around the graves.

"If you can picture the lines as I walk them, in the end they form an arrow."

It took some effort for the others to visualize it, but sure enough, the pattern of lines created an arrow pointing out from Leopold's grave.

"So we need to go that way?" Pam seemed unimpressed. "That really narrows it down."

Jay looked off to the horizon. A farmhouse rested on a hill presiding over vast fields of corn. "The crop circles," he said, a lilt of amusement in his voice. "Gotta be."

**XL259:**

Repiort your progressd.

**GeeKing:**

WUZ @ CLU SITE. GOT 411.

**XL259:**

411?

**GeeKing:**

CLUE SOLVED.

**XL259:**

Goosd. What nextr?

**GeeKing:**

NEED SOMETHING 2 READ NXT CLUE

**XL259:**

Need wjat?

**GeeKing:**

SHOULD DISCUSS F2F.

**XL259:**

What?

**GeeKing:**

FACE TO FACE. WHAT I NEED = $$$.

**XL259:**

Expensde is noit an issye.

**GeeKing:**

VBG.

**XL259:**

Wuld you wfrite like a humna beinbg?!

**GeeKing:**

AT LEAST I CAN TYPE!. VBG = VERY
BIG GRIN. :) LOL. K. 2NITE?

**XL259:**

Just nmeet me at 8.

**GeeKing:**

NP.

**XL259:**

Normakl placwe? Yes.

**GeeKing:**

NO. NP = NO PROBLEM.

**XL259:**

Meret me there!,

# CHAPTER THIRTEEN

# GOING IN CIRCLES

The Tennent Crop Circles were a well-known local attraction and one of Rockville's Seven Unnatural Wonders. All seven wonders were, in theory, created by natural phenomena. However, the fact that so many bizarre sites were located so close to one another tempted even the most skeptical of skeptics to invite the possibility that something unnatural was afoot. The Seven Unnatural Wonders were, in no particular order: the Tennent Crop Circles, the Caves of Shadows, Spooklight Forest, the Broken Brook, Swallow Falls, the Khionesian Floes, and the Cliffs of Death.

Despite the fact that the crop circles were deemed "unnatural," the ghost hunters had very little personal experience with them. In fact, Jay hadn't been there since he was eight, when he played hide-and-seek in the cornfields before being chased off by a shotgun-wielding Farmer Ed Tennent and his Rottweiler. No one was allowed on Tennent's property—unless they paid the full price of admission, that is.

It was Sunday, and tomorrow they'd have to return to school, so they needed to make the most of the day. Genevra had asked Brian to go with her to the mall, but he told her he had to go out of town with his family. Danni would have easily noted the facial tics associated with lying, but Genevra appeared far less perceptive and quickly returned her full attention to the Uggs she was planning to buy. Jay, meanwhile, told his mom he was going to study with his friends. Only Pam told the truth about where she was going—after all, if pressed, Momma could look inside her mind—though she did leave out the part about the Dominion Glass. All Momma said was, "Tell Ed Tennent he owes me five hundred bucks."

They met up just outside of the Tennent property, where Jay turned to the second page of *The Dominion Glass*. Once again, there was a poem:

> *Walk in circles*
> *Walk in circles*
> *Until your face*
> *Turns red and purple*
> *Then give up*
> *And then look down*
> *To the signal*
> *On the ground*
> *Behold the secret*
> *Of the site*
> *See it now*
> *In a whole new light*

"More walking?" Pam asked in disbelief. "This Warga guy evidently thinks exercise is very important."

Jay turned to Brian. "Any ideas?"

"I don't know," he said "It almost seems like this is referring to the last site. We walked around over and over until our faces were red and purple with frustration. Then we were about to give up, and then we looked on the ground for the arrow."

"And the arrow pointed us here." Jay reread the poem. "The clue has to mean the crop circles. It *has* to. 'Walk in circles, walk in circles.'"

"What does the EP say about crop circles?" Danni asked.

Though Jay hadn't read much on the subject of crop circles, Danni was quick to remind him that some theories about their creation included ghosts. Others suggested everything from natural events, like ball lightning and tornados, to secret military experiments. Some people claimed that the circles were UFO landing sites, but even Jay, who had seen a lot of strange things in his life, thought this explanation was ridiculous. Danni's favorite theory about crop circles came from an M. T. Boesch short story that proposed they were the result of the gods' bowel movements falling from the skies.

Jay pulled out the EP and read the entry on crop circles. Just as he was explaining about "node-wrapping," Pam glanced over at the book, squinting at the sun-drenched page. As she leaned in to get a closer look, he snapped the

# CHAPTER THIRTEEN

**Crop Circles:** Since appearing in the 1970s, crop circles have become the subject of extensive paranormal study. Some observers contend that they are created by freak meteorological phenomena, while others claim they are coded messages from extraterrestrials.

Both skeptics and believers admit that there seem to be two types of crop circles. One group of circles features undamaged plant stems that are often mysteriously woven together (node-wrapping). These circles give off increased levels of electromagnetic activity, and the soil is usually dehydrated. Whether or not the source of these circles is paranormal, science cannot yet explain them.

A second group of circles have damaged plant stems, register no changes in electromagnetic imagery, and show no dehydration in soil composition. These circles are presumed to be made by skillful hoaxers.

gleaming book shut—it was like a light turning off—and said, "Why don't we see what kind of circles we're dealing with."

"Yeah," Danni agreed. "Let's see what might"—she paused dramatically just like her favorite TV detectives—"*crop* up."

"Jeez, Danni," Brian whined. "That one was pretty—"

"I know," Danni said apologetically. "Pretty *corny*."

"Ouch," Jay winced. "Stop, please."

They walked ahead down the shoulder of the country lane, the air around them still and silent. A few crows arced across the open sky.

"Seriously, though," Danni said, looking out into the vast cornfields. "This whole place does seem kind of"—her voice was cold and ominous—"*ear-y*."

"Ugh." Pam mimed putting a gun to her head and blasting away, which only made Danni smile wider.

The dirt road that led to the Tennent property was lined with a series of billboards advertising the circles—they appeared every twenty feet or so—and little effort was made to blend them into the countryside behind them. By contrast, the Tennent farmhouse—with its three chimneys, flower boxes under each window, and wraparound front porch—looked like something you'd see in *Country Living* magazine. Inside, however, was a different story.

The farmhouse had been converted into a museum

of sorts, although "museum" suggests a hint of class and restraint. This was more like a cheesy flea market where every kind of souvenir and knickknack was available for a price: crop circle posters, calendars, puzzles, and mouse pads; little maze games where you had to maneuver a tiny silver ball from one end of the miniature plastic crop circle to the other; Paranormal Popcorn (a big seller that Ed Tennent claimed on certain days would pop itself); even T-shirts that said "I'M A-MAIZE-ING" and "I WENT TO THE TENNENT CROP CIRCLES AND ALL I GOT WAS THIS LOUSY T-SHIRT AND A SURGE OF PARANORMAL ENERGY."

Walking into the giant gift shop, Pam remembered why Ed Tennent owed Momma five hundred dollars. She had acted as a consultant for the Tennent family, not on the paranormal energies in the fields, but on how to, in Momma's words, "monetize the property." Her advice must have worked: The Tennents had built a new home, farther up on the property, a 5000-square-foot mansion—complete with a gaudy four-tractor garage and a crop-circle-shaped pool—that stuck out from the natural surroundings like a diamond-ringed sore thumb.

The gift shop wasn't the only way the Tennents cashed in on the paranormal. The store, which was run by Ed Tennent himself and his eldest daughter, Sally Sue, was the only way to gain admittance to the circles. They charged thirty dollars apiece for that privilege. And that didn't mean that each customer paid thirty dollars. It meant *both* Ed and Sally Sue Tennent charged thirty dollars, for a total of sixty dollars. You paid Sally Sue as you entered the front door, and you paid Ed as you walked out the back.

When the kids approached the ticket counter and explained that they didn't have any money, Sally Sue was unsympathetic. She looked the part of a farmer's daughter—not the pretty kind, but the kind who couldn't afford proper dental care. Her teeth were slanted and splayed in all sorts of random directions, creating huge chasms between them. Her gray eyes were dull and empty, and her auburn hair was thin and brittle like burned straw.

"It's research for a school science project," Jay told her.

"I'm shorry," Sally Sue said, spittle misting from the cracks between her teeth.

"What seems to be the pickle over here?" Ed Tennent sputtered in his jovial Southern twang as he ambled over toward the ticket counter.

"They can't pay. They shay ish for a shiensh project."

"Well, I certainly am a believer in ed-joo-cation." Farmer Tennent smiled. His teeth had fared far better than his daughter's. They gleamed white, preposterously white, and they were large and uniform. They were, in a way, an unnatural wonder all their own. In fact, Farmer Tennent's whole face was. Partially hidden by a wide-brimmed straw hat, his forehead was large and his eyes were sunken, betraying his actual age. But the rest of his face was professionally stretched, tugged, nipped, and spray-tanned, giving the illusion of a much younger man. However, when he got close, the illusion disappeared; the angles didn't look right, his eyes were pulled and devilish, and he just looked strange. Eeriest of all, nothing on his face moved as he spoke. His expression never changed.

"Of course," Farmer Tennent continued, "I never made it past grade five myself, since I had to help out on the family farm. But y'all know I just can't let y'all slide by like a greased pig on a hot Wednesday. It'd be unfair to the other customers."

"There's gotta be something you can do," Jay pleaded.

"Tell you what: I'll make it a hundred and fifty for two, cut you a deal."

"That's fifteen bucks *more* for each person," Brian said immediately.

"Is it?" Farmer Tennent asked. "I never was good with numbers, but I can yank a turnip out of dried cement, tell you what."

"You owe my mom five hundred bucks," Pam snapped. Then, losing patience, she looked at Ed's dopey frozen grin and said, "Why don't you just drop the whole—" Jay stamped on her foot. "Ow!"

"Look, Farmer Tennent," Jay reasoned, and the others could swear they heard a country drawl creeping into his voice. "I'm just a simple twelve-year-old. Like you as a youngster, I've been on my own since I stumbled my first steps. We're two peas in a pod, we are—both of us left to fend for ourselves like a... uh, lamb in, uh, a... sweater shop. Anyway, while we can't pay your very reasonable admission fee, we can offer you something more valuable."

"Now, son, what could be more valuable than the harvest of beautiful, green fifty dollar bills?"

"Publicity."

Farmer Tennent raised the brim of his straw hat as Jay continued, "Pam can talk to Momma Petrucci and have her tag an advertisement onto her astrological blog."

"Momma's blog, huh?"

"She gets ten thousand views a month."

"Uniques or total hits?" Farmer Tennent asked, his stretched face revealing the maniacal glint gathering in his unblinking eyes.

"Wow, pretty smart there for a simple country farmer," Jay said, his own expression just as still and steady. "Either way, Momma's readers are your target audience. Also, Brian here is the most popular kid in school. He talks about the circles, and then every kid is going to want to come here. With six hundred kids in our school, that's…"

"Three thousand six hundred dollars before tax," Brian said. "Not counting siblings."

"Now, I'm having trouble following the snakes and ladders of all your fancy words and nimble numbers, but I think I catch your drift in my own simpleminded way." Farmer Tennent turned to Sally Sue. "Tell you what, Sal, go ahead and let these kind folks through, would you?"

"Excuse me," Danni said as they walked by a display of crop-circle-inspired earrings. "Do you mind if I ask you a question?"

"Sure, but I'm not much of an answer man."

"Just between you and me," she winked. "Did you make these circles yourself? They're brilliantly constructed."

"Well, dear me." He looked her squarely in the eye. "I certainly did not. I awoke one day and they were just there." And with that, Farmer Tennent walked off to hard-sell a case of Paranormal Popcorn to a family of four.

"That was genius," Pam said to Jay as they left the Tennents' back door and began walking down the first cornstalk-bordered path.

"Make sure Momma mentions him in her blog," Jay told her. "And tell her to make it a scathing review."

"He wasn't lying, by the way," Danni said, already snapping pictures of the fields. "Solid eye contact, no blinking, speech didn't speed up. He may be a con man, but he definitely did *not* create these circles."

The corn on either side of the path was dense and tall, a good two feet taller than they were—Ed Tennent claimed that spirit energy was a natural fertilizer—and the path itself wasn't really a path, but rather cobbled with short, bent cornstalks, which made walking difficult. (Of course, like the rest of the guests, they had to sign a waiver declaring that the Tennents were not responsible for injuries suffered on the property.)

At about two hundred yards, the path fed into a large perfect circle with a diameter of thirty feet or so. Beyond it were two other circles.

"So where do we go?" Brian asked. "The clue just says to walk in the circles. Which ones?"

Jay stood on his toes, trying to see over the corn. "I'm not sure."

"These stalks are bent and broken," Danni said, kneeling down with her head nearly touching the ground. "No node-wrapping, no weaving pattern."

"Interesting." Jay whipped out his EMF detector and placed it just above the broken stalks. "No electromagnetic activity, either."

They were starting to get looks from tourists. A chubby kid in a hat with a foam cornstalk sticking up from the top stared at them through goofy crop-circle-shaped novelty glasses. Unconcerned, Danni reached down and grabbed a handful of dirt. "This soil is definitely not dehydrated," she said.

Now the chubby kid's entire chubby family was eyeing her curiously. Both Pam and Brian were envious of Danni, the way she didn't care at all what others thought about her. She did what she wanted, she liked what she liked, and she said what she thought. This behavior normally would be social suicide for a sixth grader, but with her bright, impish face and unwaveringly cheerful approach to life, Danni somehow got away with it.

She'd been like that for as long as anyone could remember. At age three, Danni discovered a dead chameleon while digging in the sandbox. By naptime, she had used her preschool's most advanced technological innovations (plastic rakes, shovels, and pails) to conduct her first forensic investigation. Oblivious to other kids' curious stares, she happily cordoned off the sandbox with a streamer from the school's Halloween decorations.

Two years later, in kindergarten, she received her first report card. In the comments section, her teacher had written: "Danni plays well with others, shares readily, and is extremely considerate and polite. She does, however, display a strange fascination with rodents, fungi, and, most of all, insects, going so far as to suggest that the class adopt a tick she found as the school mascot."

When she brought in her home's bug zapper for show-and-tell, the school's humorless vice principal, Mr. Fahrner, called in Danni's parents for a conference. "What do you have to say about this?" Mr. Fahrner asked them accusingly as he handed them the bug zapper.

"Well," Mrs. Besner said, staring into the bag of insects, "that honeybee would have died shortly anyway. You can tell because its stinger is missing."

"That's right," Mr. Besner agreed, peering into the plastic bag. "And look at that," he said, smiling the same innocuous smile as his daughter, "a scarab larva has hatched. It's been surviving on the Japanese beetle carcasses." He handed the bag back to Mr. Fahrner, who stared back at them, silent and slack-jawed. To be fair, how was he supposed to know that the Besners were both nationally recognized professors of entomology, having recently scored the coveted Golden Arthropod prize for a *Journal of Insect Science* article entitled "Odor Proliferation in the German Cockroach"?

And so it wasn't surprising that, years later, Danni stared into the maze of mashed cornstalks, distracted by a colony of ants, each one carrying a loose kernel of corn nearly twice its size.

"Danni, come on!" Jay stood at the opening to the second circle. "How long can you stare at the ground?"

Danni's personal record for staring at the ground was over four hours—when she had examined the intricacies in the pattern of a sneaker print—but there were more pressing issues at hand than ants, so she hopped up and scuttled ahead to join the others.

By the end of the day, they had walked through all of the crop circles. Unfortunately, they found nothing anywhere that remotely resembled a clue. They turned to leave just as the sun set over the forest of corn. A red glow cast over the circles, and the corncobs blossomed like a field of wildflowers.

That night, before he went to bed, Jay read the poem over and over. He read it out loud. He read it backward. He read it out of order. Then he scoured the Internet for hours, looking for anything related to the phrases in the poem. He was about to power off the computer when he saw that Pam was online and clicked to start a video chat.

"Jay, it's past midnight," she said.

"So then why are you online?"

"Dad brought home this handkerchief that's evidence in his case. Momma told me to go to my room and hold it until I get some kind of vision. Her exact words were, 'Even if it takes all night.'"

"So you're looking for something online to fake it?"

"Yep. It's a red silk handkerchief with the initials GM. I found something about a magician named the Great Mazzini."

"That's not bad."

"Until they realize I'm wrong."

Jay held open *The Dominion Glass* up to the computer's camera. "I've been looking for something about the poem. But I'm not finding anything."

"Jay, put that away!" Pam exclaimed. "We're not supposed to be talking about it."

"They just said phone and e-mail."

"I'm sure they meant this too."

"Just real quick, ask the spirit board."

"Come on, Jay."

"Just ask, 'How can we get the next clue?'"

In the video chat window on Jay's monitor, Pam's picture suddenly jolted askew. "Fine," she sighed, and the picture began to shake as Jay heard the thumps of Pam's feet against her stairs. The picture stilled, and Jay's monitor showed the Petruccis' spirit board kitchen table.

"Can you see my hands?" she asked.

"Tilt it up a little."

"Good?"

"Yeah, perfect."

Pam closed her eyes and took a deep breath. She

began her routine, but Jay could tell she was just going through the motions. "Creatures of the Spirit World, guide my hands." She lowered her voice. "But keep it down since my parents are sleeping… Anyway, Spirits of the Great Beyond, fill me with your energy… blah, blah, blah… guide my hands, oh, awesome spirits… yada, yada, yada… just tell us how to get the next clue on our quest."

Jay watched on his monitor as Pam's hands scurried about the table in a pattern that was becoming all too familiar: the letters P, M, and A.

"You happy now?" Pam said, thrusting the planchette away in disgust.

"It was worth a try."

"That's it, Jay. Next time, if you want some advice about the future, consult a fortune cookie." She stood up from the table. "Now, if you'll excuse me, I have to hold a stranger's used handkerchief for the rest of the night."

As preoccupied as he was, Jay couldn't help chuckling as Pam's video window disappeared. He closed his laptop, plopped down on his bed, and grabbed the digital recorder from his backpack. He dictated into it: "Investigated Tennent Crop Circles. No evidence of node-wrapping. No EMF activity. Plan is to return to crop circles and investigate further."

He tossed the recorder on the nightstand, lay down, and closed his eyes. It took him a while to get to sleep, and when he did, it was fitful again, full of tossing and turning and a messy montage of dreams. Jay dreamed he was back

in the cornfield and the Paranormal Popcorn was popping off the stalks. Figures emerged from the corn, walking out from the tall stalks into the clearings of the circles: Brian, Danni, Pam, Momma Petrucci, all their teachers from school, the librarians, and, finally, his dad. They all circled around him and held hands. They began to spin, and Jay tried to stay focused on his dad, but he lost him, and the faces became a whirling merry-go-round. When the circle stopped, the faces were all replaced with Farmer Tennent's surgically doctored mug.

"It's not our place to interfere," the thirty Ed Tennents said in a unified twang. "We mean, we're just simple country farmers. Searching for the glass is like trying to catch a greased grouse with oven mitts on. What say you let it go, huh?"

The Farmer Tennent clones walked toward him creepily, arms outstretched, teeth gleaming. Jay was trapped. Then a rooster crowed, and he saw the ceiling of his bedroom.

As he awoke, the phony country tone of Farmer Tennent's synchronized voices still rang in his head and made him sick. He was suddenly worried that he and his friends were at a dead end on the hunt for the Dominion Glass. And now he had to go to school and pretend to be interested in diagramming sentences, all the while thinking about the quest, his father, and clues in a cornfield. The day was starting out on a bad note.

But then he noticed that *The Dominion Glass* was open on his nightstand. Once again, the pneumaticles rested on top. He slipped them on and took a look at the page. The ghostwriter had struck again.

Walk in circles,

Walk in circles

Until your face

Turns red and purple

Then give up

And then look down

To the signal

On the ground

Behold the secret

Of the site

See it now

In a whole new light

# CHAPTER FOURTEEN

## LETTERS IN THE NIGHT

That morning in school, all of the ghost hunters had trouble concentrating. Not only were they stumped by the riddle of the crop circles, but a ghost had once more visited Jay in the middle of the night and offered another clue—a clue that didn't make any sense.

Pam was so distracted that she missed fourteen out of twenty questions on a math quiz; Jay absentmindedly wrote "corn" on a history test to answer the question "Who was the third president?"; and Danni stared off into space during a gym class dodgeball game and was consequently beaned in the head by, of all people, a newly confident Seth. Worst of all, Brian was so preoccupied with figuring out the riddle of the crop circles that he forgot to get any questions wrong on his vocabulary test and received a 100 percent. His English teacher, Mrs. Unseld, commended him by saying, "See, there's hope for all of us!"

At lunch, when Danni, Pam, and Jay got up to throw their trash away, Brian took the opportunity to leave the popular table and join them. He spoke to the others without actually making eye contact as he scooped scraps of spaghetti from his tray into a nearby garbage can. Genevra looked at him every so often, but he ignored her, trying to act like throwing his lunch away demanded strict concentration.

"So what does OVF stand for?" Brian asked them, his eyes firmly focused on the spaghetti he was dumping, strand by strand, into the trash. "Is it in the EP?"

"No." Jay put the pneumaticles on and looked at the message. "It's weird. The writing is messy, like the ghost was rushing."

"Dude, take those off," Brian said sharply. "People are going to wonder why you suddenly need glasses."

Jay looked up at Brian quizzically. "Relax. They're just glasses."

"They just...," Brian stammered, "...they just draw attention."

"What do you care?" Pam said. "You're not even talking to us. You're busy breaking the world record for longest time to dispose of a tray of pasta."

"Speaking of which, I'm out of trash," he said. "Let's meet in the lab after school."

Mr. Linkins was dissecting what was left of a frog when the young ghost hunters scurried into his room. "So what sort of supernatural silliness do I need to dispel today?" he asked, moving his goggles up on his forehead.

As soon as they mentioned the crop circles to him, he made his opinion known: "Lies! All lies."

Mr. Linkins jogged to the lab's closet, dragged out one of dozens of boxes full of random papers, books, and lab equipment, and started digging into it. "Crop circles are hoaxes," he said, rifling through the box until he found what he was looking for. "Aha!" He pulled out an issue of *National Skeptic* magazine. The cover showed two men standing in a cornfield, each of them holding a large piece of plywood. The headline read, "Crop Circles a Crock!"

He handed Jay the magazine and flipped past an article that refuted Bigfoot sightings to a cover story that reported how two British hoaxers made dozens of crop circles using wooden planks, rope, and wire.

"And yet still some people have the moxie to claim that crop circles are UFO landing sites," Mr. Linkins said with a laugh.

"I know, right?" Jay agreed.

"But that doesn't mean they're all hoaxes," Danni said. "Real crop circles show node-wrapping—"

"There are no such things as real crop circles," Mr. Linkins interrupted. "Some are just more cleverly conceived. I guarantee those circles were man-made. In fact…" He began rummaging through another box and plucked out some photos with a satisfied look on his face. "…I can prove it."

He handed them the photographs. The pictures were shot from far away with a zoom lens, so the resolution wasn't perfect, but they were clear enough to show a group of people using planks and ropes to mash down shapes in the cornfields. In the background was the Tennents' original farmhouse.

"There's your proof," Mr. Linkins said triumphantly as Jay sorted through the pictures.

"Did you take these?" Danni asked.

"I don't remember how I got them. Skeptics are always exchanging information."

"Who are these people?" Jay wondered out loud. "It's not the Tennents."

Pam looked through the photos. "So somebody does it as a prank, and then the Tennents make the most of an opportunity."

"That would explain how Ed Tennent wasn't lying when he said he awoke one day to find them," Danni added.

"Are these people part of the OVF, maybe?" Brian inquired.

"The what?" Mr. Linkins asked, suddenly interested.

Jay looked at him and nearly spilled everything, but thought better of it. A skeptic like Mr. Linkins would have laughed them out of the room if Jay explained the whole ghostwriting thing. Plus, the quest was top secret.

"Can I hang on to these, Mr. Linkins?" Jay asked, squinting to try to find a recognizable face in the blurry photograph.

Mr. Linkins shrugged. "I don't see why not. Everyone knows it's a hoax."

As Jay led his friends from the room, Mr. Linkins added one more thing: "If you ask me, I'd keep some distance from the circles. You're all above this sort of nonsense."

"So it's a hoax," Jay said as they walked down the hall. "These pictures prove it. I guess we go back the Tomb of the Eight Brothers and look for something else." He reached into his pocket and pulled out his recorder. He brought it up to his lips and was about to hit the record button when he suddenly stopped. "Oh, man."

"What?" Brian asked.

"I left this recording all night." He hit the rewind button. "This is going to take forever."

"Stop," Danni said.

Jay stopped walking. "Why?"

"I mean hit stop!" She reached over and pushed the button.

"What?"

"There was a ghost in your house last night."

"Yeah?"

"So maybe you recorded it." Danni smiled, and her freckles lit up her face like stars.

"Play it back," Brian said.

"We won't hear EVP on that," Danni said. "It's too soft."

She grabbed Jay's recorder and darted down the hall. The others ran after her. They knew exactly where she was going.

When Jay, Pam, and Brian entered the music room,

Danni had already hooked up the recorder to the sound system. The state-of-the-art system—which consisted of a computer, a mixing board, an amplifier, and a set of noise-canceling headphones—was grotesquely out of place among the otherwise underfunded music program's instruments: woodblocks, triangles, a xylophone with more than half of its bars missing, and one old, rusty piccolo.

Unfortunately, the only one who actually used the equipment with any regularity was Danni, and her use was strictly nonmusical. By now, she was an expert at the sound-editing software, having employed the programs to authenticate recordings, amplify background noise, and, most importantly, isolate spirits' electronic voice phenomena.

Jay had recorded over six hours, so they each took a shift listening with the headphones. After a while, they became delirious with boredom and started to fool with the music room's instruments while they waited.

"Tah, tah, tee-tee, tah," Brian said as he tapped on a woodblock.

"You have a remarkable ability to avoid any rhythm whatsoever," Pam said, picking up the piccolo and playing a perfect set of scales before spitting out a couple of flakes of rust.

"Quiet!" Jay exclaimed, waving at them furiously. He clamped the headphones tightly to his ears.

"Do you hear something?" Pam asked, rushing over to the computer.

Jay changed the Audio Out feature from "headphones" to "system." He clicked on the editing timeline, and the sound sizzled from the speakers. After a few seconds, they heard what sounded like air releasing from a deflating tire.

"Was that a voice?" Jay said.

"Sounds like the wind," Pam said dismissively.

"It wasn't windy last night."

"You need to isolate the sound from the room tone," Danni said.

Danni reached over and moved and clicked the mouse so quickly it looked like she was playing a video game. The background hum faded away, and they heard a faint, whispery gasp.

"*Ohhh-vwahhh…*"

"Slow it down." Jay leaned into the speaker.

Danni clicked, dragged, and toggled.

"*Ohhhher-vwahhhrr…*" the speaker gasped. The voice was deep and distorted.

"Sounds like *au revoir.*" Brian said. "It means 'goodbye' in French."

"Maybe you were talking in your sleep," Pam said to Jay.

"In *French?*" Jay said, bewildered. "I don't speak French." He furrowed his brow and lifted his backpack onto a table. He removed *The Dominion Glass*, slipped on the pneumaticles, and turned to the crop circle poem. "So the ghost writes 'OVF,' but then says 'au revoir'?"

"Doesn't add up," Brian said, tapping on the wood block.

Pam was silent. She stared at the book over Jay's shoulder, her eyes burrowing into the page.

"Pam?" Brian swiped his hand in front of her face, but she didn't flinch. "*Hello? Pam?* Are you practicing your gaze again or something?"

She spoke quietly, as if she didn't want them to hear her. "I think I can see some ghostwriting."

"I know. It says 'OVF.'" Jay looked back at the book. "Wait, you mean without the glasses?"

"Not all of it. But some."

Jay looked over his shoulder and up at Pam, who was staring at the page with a combination of fear and curiosity—like someone spotting a bear in the woods. This wasn't like her. She was always downplaying her abilities, not bragging about them.

"In your encyclopedia, I saw writing on some of the pages," she continued, finally meeting Jay's eyes. "Turn to the poltergeist page. I think it might explain who's writing in your book."

"A dream ghost," Jay muttered thoughtfully after he read the ghostwriting for a second time. "No wonder I never heard anything."

"What do you mean?" Danni asked, still fiddling with the computer.

"The only way the ghost can be there is if I'm asleep."

"Oh, yeah. Duh," she said.

"So who is it then?" Brian asked, twirling the wood-

**Pockets of Purgatory:** Located in caves, forests, and other unpopulated areas, pockets of purgatory (POPs) are places where the ghosts of murderers, thieves, and other such sinners are sentenced to reside, their souls having been deemed unfit for passage to the Other Side.

As penance for the hate with which they chose to live, the ghosts are cursed to feel the resentment of other similarly despicable spirits around them, inspiring in one another a constant, immeasurable anger. Because of this curse, if a mortal happens upon purgatory ghosts, he too will be beset with a hideous anger. Within minutes, the rage becomes all-consuming, the victim is frozen, and the ghost will claim its prey (see Purgatory Ghost Paralysis, page 260). The victim's soul is then trapped in the POP, doomed to eternal imprisonment surrounded by the company of his murderers.

**Poltergeist:** Though the word "poltergeist" comes from the German meaning "noisy spirit," a poltergeist is neither a spirit nor a ghost. A poltergeist is not the presence of the spirit of the deceased, but rather the result of a living person's emotional stress. If a person is experiencing powerful emotions without a proper outlet to express them, the individual's anxiety, fear, and sadness are projected into the environment. Typical poltergeist disruptions include strange noises, electrical disturbances, and objects moving about as if under their own power. The key is not to give a poltergeist fear or anxiety. If a poltergeist cannot draw off these emotions, it loses strength and eventually fades away.

**Posing:** Posing is a slang term for ghosts pretending to be living people. Most paranormal scholars believe it is a rare occurrence. However, some ghost hunters

259

block mallet in his hand. "Was anyone in both dreams?"

Jay thought for a minute. His eyes brightened well beyond the legal blue limit. "My dad," he said. "My dad was in both dreams."

He looked down at the book and ran his fingers over the ghostwritten letters. Slowly around the "O"… down and up the "V"….

"It makes sense," Danni said, excited. "Your dad's ghost is trying to help us. He's writing the clues."

As Jay traced his finger across the horizontal lines of the "F," his eyes suddenly dimmed. His father's ghost had said goodbye. Why? Because he'd never had the chance? And did this mean that he was moving on to—Jay's heart sank with the thought—the Other Side?

Jay had shed enough tears in his twelve years to recognize all the signs: His chest tightened. His teeth hurt. Everything felt thick and sticky. He turned away from his friends, walked over toward the music room's lone window, and stared out across the soccer field. Behind the field's chain-link fence, trees swayed in the breeze, and Jay's mind drifted and stewed with a thousand questions.

"Did your dad have anything to do with a group called the OVF?" Brian asked from across the room, unaware that Jay was fighting back tears.

It took a moment for Jay to answer. "Not that I remember," he said, still staring out the window.

"What was your dad doing in your dreams?" Danni asked.

"Not much," Jay said, and he tried to replay the dreams in his head. "I mean, he was only there for a few seconds really." He suddenly turned back around and streaked back to the book, nearly rolling his ankle on the piccolo now lying on the floor.

"What?" Brian asked as Jay grabbed the pneumaticles.

"If my dad was in my dreams for just a few seconds, maybe he didn't get to finish what he was writing."

"But no word starts with 'OVF,'" Brian pointed out.

Jay's eyes narrowed and the crease in his forehead deepened. "No, but some begin 'OVE.'" He unfolded the pneumaticles and hooked them over his ears, studying the ghostwriting again. He had missed it the first time: There was a small trace of a line at the bottom of the "F," the beginning of the final foot that would turn the letter "F" into an "E."

"Oven?" Pam threw out when Jay relayed his discovery.

"*Oven?*" Brian smirked. "What are we gonna do, microwave the popcorn?"

"We had to put the first letter in the oven, didn't we?" Pam quickly retorted. She looked down at the page. Was that a circle around a word?

"Over," Brian said. "We're not supposed to go through the circles, but—"

"—*up* and *over* them!" Pam finished.

Danni clamped one headphone to her left ear and turned a few knobs on the amp. "The ghost was saying 'over,'" she said, "not 'au revoir.'"

"That makes more sense," Jay said. "My dad didn't speak French."

"So he wasn't saying goodbye after all," Pam said.

Jay shook his head. "No." And with that, his heart lifted and his eyes beamed bright blue again behind the pneumaticles.

"So how do we get over the crop circles?" Pam asked. "Should I get my private jet?"

"Balloons," Jay said, stuffing the pneumaticles into his front pocket.

*"Cool,"* Danni said. "Wait, what?"

"The Tennents offer hot-air balloon rides to view the circles," Jay replied.

"I think the 'up and over' thing is only part of it," Brian said, hunched over *The Dominion Glass*. The tip of the woodblock mallet scrolled across the poem's final lines. "Behold the secret of the site… See it now in a whole new light," Brian read aloud. "Remember at sunset the way the light from the sun fell on part of the circles? I think we should go up during sunset and see what we see."

"Until your face turns red and purple," Jay said.

"Exactly!"

As they walked—it was almost a run, really—along the sandy country lane, the Tennent Crop Circle billboards began to blur together in a jumble of slogans, numbers, and caricatures of Farmer Tennent's otherworldly face: "CORNCOB PIPES $15!"; "START YOUR DAY OFF RIGHT

WITH PARANORMAL CORNFLAKES"; "CROP CIRCLE CHILD'S PASS: HALF-PRICE" (as they passed by the sign, they saw the fine-print: "TWO-MINUTE MAXIMUM. $40 PER MINUTE THEREAFTER").

Not that they would have paid the billboards more attention if they had been walking any slower. They had far too much on their minds, especially Jay.

"How do you think your dad knows what we're up to?" Danni asked in her innocent yet brutally direct way. "And what we need help on and everything?"

"I don't know," Jay said. He had been wondering the same thing from the moment they'd bolted from the music room.

"Well, he is *in your head*," Pam said as they passed by a billboard that read, "A CORNucopia of wonder awaits!" "Momma always says our dreams are our subconscious mind trying to solve problems. So your dad is kind of part of that, if you think about it."

Something about the way Pam said "He is *in your head*" bothered Jay. Though, if the EP's ghostwriting was right—and he had no reason to doubt that it was—what she was saying was true. The ghostwriting had described a dream ghost as "not the ghost exactly, but an echo of the spirit." Did that mean it wasn't really his dad's ghost, the way a poltergeist wasn't really a ghost? He wished Dr. Grunspan was around to ask about all of this.

Every question led to another. Was the dream ghost different from the one he'd seen in the forest? Was it all in his head like Pam was suggesting? Then again, the ghostwriting said that a dream ghost wasn't exactly like a poltergeist—it was a hybrid. And Brian had explained to all of them that "hybrid" means "mixture." "Like the way a hybrid car runs on both gas and electricity," Brian had pompously told them. And then he launched into some long-winded explanation of the word's origin that just made it easier for Jay's thoughts to wander to his father.

Pam, meanwhile, was filtering the recent events through a veil of self-doubt the way only she could. Yes, she could see ghostwriting—that much was clear. Not all of it, and not all of the time, but she could do what it appeared no one else could. For the briefest of moments, this made her happy; it was something not normal, something *ab*normal, something *paranormal*. But then she started thinking… and thinking… and thinking: about how Momma didn't seem to think it was worth exploring. About how Darla was reading tea leaves at a tenth-grade level when she was Pam's age. About how this wasn't actually psychic at all, it was just weird. In the end, she just felt like more of a freak than ever. Why couldn't she do something conventionally paranormal, something traditionally mystical, something… *normally* abnormal, just once?

"Let's see," Farmer Tennent said, "four individuals for a hot-air balloon ride, at a hundred dollars apiece… I'll give you a deal for seven hundred dollars."

They stared coldly at the farmer. A blinding grin

plastered on his face, he continued, "There's my learning disability again." He cleared his throat. "Of course, if you have something to offer a hurting farm like ours… maybe a month-long banner ad on Momma Petrucci's blog linked to our e-commerce site."

"How about we *don't* publish the pictures we have of hoaxers creating the fields?" Jay suggested. He pulled out the pictures that Mr. Linkins had given them. As he fanned the photos for Farmer Tennent to see, Jay felt like he was showing a winning poker hand.

Ed Tennent looked surprised (at least as much as his fixed expression would allow), and Danni could tell his reaction was genuine. In fact, Farmer Ed was so shocked by the discovery of the photos, he waved the group ahead to the balloon with no charge.

The balloon ride was run by Farmer Ed's oldest son, Bobbie Bill Tennent, known to most as Double B. Double B didn't look or act like the rest of his family; he was tall, had chiseled features, and wore small, oval glasses that complemented his thoughtful expression. "Up and away we go," he said, sounding bored.

Double B pumped a lever, activating the burner, and flames gasped into the balloon, causing it to rise. They slowly floated up above the house and toward the cornfields. The farmhouse and barns soon speckled the ground like little LEGO buildings, and before long, they were looking down on the entirety of the crop circle patterns.

Once they had reached a certain height, Double B

turned off the burner and let the balloon drift. He pulled out a copy of William Shakespeare's *Romeo and Juliet* and began reading, while they stared down at the circles looking for some sort of clue.

"Is there going to be another arrow?" Pam asked.

"Maybe it'll spell something," Jay said.

"Not unless it's 'Ooo,'" Danni said, leaning over the basket to take an aerial photo. "It's pretty much just circles."

Double B didn't seem particularly interested in the unusual comments. "Ready to go down?" he asked after twenty minutes, not bothering to look up from his book.

"Hold on. We'd like to see the beautiful sunset from here," Pam said, brushing her bangs behind her ears and smiling.

Brian whispered mockingly in her ear, "Are you actually trying to flirt with him?"

"Shut up or I'll throw you over the basket," she said through the corner of her smile, as fake and frozen as Farmer Ed's.

Just then, the sun hit the horizon, and a red-purple ray blanketed a portion of the ground below. Like a highlighter, it colored a piece of the circle patterns. Everybody noticed it except Pam, whose glance still lingered on Double B.

"Whoa. That can't be coincidence," Brian said.

Pam stopped staring dreamily at Double B and looked down to the fields. "What do you mean?" she asked Brian.

"That's the symbol I saw in the crystal ball."

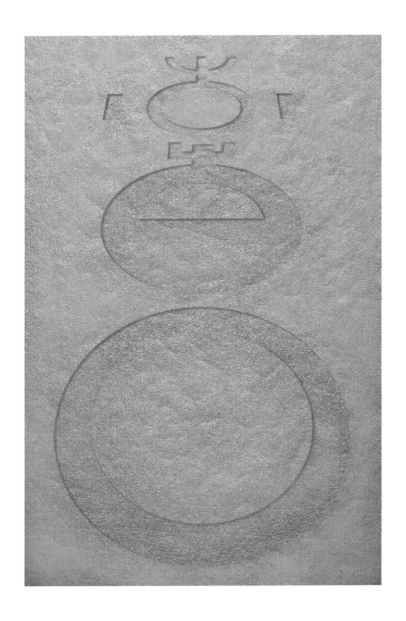

"The people in those pictures." Jay said as a light breeze picked up. "They must have been the ones who hid the Dominion Glass. They made these circles as a clue."

Double B lifted his thoughtful eyes from the pages of his book. Unfortunately, he had no time to inquire about the strange statement as a UFO was quickly approaching, coming at them as if fired from the gun barrel of the crimson sun.

# CHAPTER FIFTEEN

# A SIGN OF THE TIMES

The flying object went from unidentified to terrifying in the span of about ten seconds—oval body, angled tail, spinning propeller.

As the helicopter neared—showing absolutely no sign of stopping—Jay made out two figures in its cockpit. One was a strong-jawed pilot with flight goggles strapped across his face; the other was Jonathan Pross.

"What the?" Double B tugged at the balloon's ropes, frantically trying to steer out of the helicopter's path. "He's heading right for us!"

Just when it seemed a collision was imminent, the helicopter slowed to a stop. It hovered, barely a stone's throw away, and turned broadside. A door opened behind the cockpit, and out poked Pross's smirking face.

"WHAT ARE YOU KIDS DOING HERE?" he shouted over the chopper's near-deafening growl.

Below them, cornstalks swayed in the swirling wind.

"JUST TAKING A BALLOON RIDE," Jay shouted back. "FOR FUN."

Pross screeched to be heard over the noise: "BALLOONS ARE SUCH A PRIMITIVE WAY TO TRAVEL," he yelled, and even when shouting he sounded smug. "THEY'RE SO…" His smirk wriggled like a centipede. "…VULNERABLE TO THE ELEMENTS."

The helicopter edged forward. The wind from its propeller dimpled the balloon's side.

"LEAVE US ALONE," Jay commanded. "THIS DOESN'T CONCERN YOU."

"YOU HAVE THAT BACKWARD," Pross shouted. "IT DOESN'T CONCERN *YOU*."

The helicopter dipped suddenly. As it turned away, its tail propeller nipped the balloon, slashing a jagged gash through the nylon. The balloon sputtered air, and the basket lurched violently. Everybody tumbled within it like dice rattling in a cup.

The calm, studious look on Double B's face gave way to something between concern and panic. He pumped the fire in rapid bursts, trying to breathe some life back into the balloon. But when the nylon collapsed dangerously close to the flames, he stopped pumping. In a resigned voice, barely audible over the helicopter's hum, he gulped, "Hold on."

"OMG," Pross said in a mockingly plain tone. "You're crashing."

Pross's whiny voice trailed away as they plummeted toward the ground. The basket twisted and turned with the balloon's last breaths until—*whack*—it slammed against the cornstalks. The sky went black. The deflating balloon draped over them. Everyone scrambled madly to escape, for fear of being smothered.

As Jay crawled out from under the dying balloon, he saw something through the gap between two rows of corn: a red blur, about twenty yards away. He pushed aside the stem of a cornstalk to get a better view. Someone was out there, staring at them through binoculars. Confused, Jay looked up past the corncobs and saw Pross's helicopter hovering off into the fiery horizon. When he looked back through the corn, the spy was gone.

"Everyone okay?" Double B asked, getting to his feet.

"Define 'okay,'" Pam groaned as he pulled her up from the ground.

"You're bleeding," he said, dabbing her forehead. A spot of blood appeared on his finger.

Pam felt dizzy—it had been quite a fall.

"Let me see," Danni said, stepping over the mashed stalks. "That's nothing." She sounded disappointed. "Probably won't even leave a scar."

Jay looked back out to the horizon. The helicopter was a dot in the distance. Its dull roar faded to a murmur, and then, finally, to silence.

As they walked away from the farm, Jay followed blindly

a few yards behind the others, his head buried in *The Dominion Glass*. The pneumaticles clung to the tip of his nose. "I don't see the symbol in here," he said. "But the next page does seem to hint to it. It says, 'Now that you have seen your sign... Take a visit back in time... Find the voice to set you free... And lead you to the special key.'"

"Jay, can we just chill out for a minute?" Pam said drowsily from up ahead.

"Pross saw the symbol too. We don't have time to *chill out*," he said.

Pam stopped and turned around so abruptly that dust kicked up from the road. "Jay!" she cried in disbelief. "He just tried to kill us!"

"That might have been an accident."

"That was not an accident!"

"Well, then all the more reason to figure out what that symbol is before he does."

Pam shook her head in frustration. "Are you *serious*?" A strand of hair stuck to the trickle of blood just above her brow. "We just almost died. *Again*. Don't you think it's about time we stop this insane quest?!"

"The symbol is a clue," Jay said, becoming agitated. "I'm sure of it!" He turned to Brian. "Bri, can you decode this?"

Brian looked off into the gray sky, now studded with the evening's first stars. "Dude, she's right," he said. "We might not be so lucky next time."

Jay huffed, exasperated, and turned to Danni. "Danni?"

"Sorry, Jay," she said. She tried to smile. "I'm all for investigating dead bodies, but that doesn't mean I want to become one."

"We tried," Pam sighed. "But enough is enough, Jay. Let it go."

Jay clamped the book shut and stuffed it into his backpack. "I can't believe you guys," he muttered, mostly to himself.

Then he shot ahead, quickly pulling away from the others, until he was lost in darkness, and night took over.

**GeeKing:**
I HAVE NXT CLUE

**XL259:**
Good. And tge kids?

**GeeKing:**
THEM 2, BUT I THINK I SCARED
THEM OFF.

**XL259:**
Don"t assuyme anythinog.

**GeeKing:**
I'LL MMS THE SYMBOL

**XL259:**
Mms?

**GeeKing:**
MESSAGE THE GRAPHIC

**XL259:**
I don"t klnow how to work taht.

**GeeKing:**

SENT

**XL259:**

Juyst brimg it to me! How casn thwse kids be ahead of yoiu?

**GeeKing:**

IDK.

**XL259:**

Who is IDK?

**GeeKing:**

I DON'T KNOW.

**XL259:**

Thenm why did yoiu type it?

**GeeKing:**

LOL IDK STANDS FOR I DON'T KNOW CUL8R

Pam was waiting just inside the door when Jay approached the entrance to school the following day. "Jay," she called out to him.

He glanced at her with the same blend of contempt and disregard that Genevra usually employed.

"Jay, wait."

"I have to get to class," he said, rushing by her.

Pam grabbed his backpack, and he snapped back toward her.

"What do you want?" he said impatiently.

"Look, we're sorry about bailing on—" It was two

minutes until the morning bell, and only a handful of kids clustered in the front hall, but they were close enough to hear her. "—you know, the assignment."

"Glad you're sorry." He started off again.

Pam grabbed his arm. She leaned in and lowered her voice. "You know, you might want to think about it a little more before you go putting your life in reckless danger."

He pulled away from her. "We gave our word to the librarians."

"Jay, you're just a kid. Don't you think they'd understand?"

"You don't understand," he blurted out, his muscles tensing.

"Me? What are you—"

"You don't understand that this might be the only chance I have to find my father!"

It was hard to tell who was more surprised at Jay's sudden outburst: Pam, or Jay himself. The few straggling students in the hall looked over at them, mumbled uncomfortably, and then walked away. The two ghost hunters stood in the hallway alone, staring at each other. Jay was breathing heavily—red-faced, his temples throbbing—as if he had just finished a sprint. A dying fluorescent light flickered above them.

"You're right," Pam finally said quietly, "I don't understand." She blinked, and there was that warm look so unbefitting for a psychic.

Jay thought about telling her the truth, what had been

brewing in his mind ever since he read about the Dominion Glass—how he could keep it for himself and somehow figure out how to use it to summon his father. But instead, he looked back over his shoulder to see if anyone was still near, and then turned back and said, "If we find the glass, we'll become members of the Association. We'll have access to all of their tools and all of their wisdom. And then maybe…" He looked down at the hall's shining tiles. "Then maybe they can help me find my father."

The bell rang, but neither of them moved. Pam tried to read Jay's expression, but he bowed his head even further, burying his chin in his chest.

"I better go," she said. "If I'm late for social studies, Mrs. Turak will give me detention. And then Momma will be mad and say I should have seen it coming and everything."

The top of Jay's head barely shook, and Pam ran off, nearly slipping as she raced around a corner.

*What a waste of time,* Jay thought as he finally looked up into the deserted hall. They weren't teaching him anything useful here. How was learning to simplify fractions going to help him crack the latest clue? How would knowing about photosynthesis help him find his father's ghost? It was pointless—all of it. The last thing he felt like doing right now was studying.

So he turned around and headed straight to the school library.

The school's library was a far cry from the city's

esteemed historic institution. The entire library spanned less than half the size of a tennis court, it was only one level, and there were far fewer books—most of which had been defiled with immature student comments or had pages missing (torn out for spitball ammo).

The school librarian, Mrs. Heifitz, didn't measure up to the public library's standards either. For one thing, she wasn't a kung-fu-savvy secret agent of an ancient order dedicated to preserving paranormal secrets. And for another, she was really annoying. At the moment, her annoyingness was ruining his concentration. He sat at the library's computer, Googling unsuccessfully for something related to the symbol. Nearby, Mrs. Heifitz reclined at her desk, feet kicked up, talking on her cell phone. Loudly.

"I'm not sure we want to let her into the chapter," she raved into the phone as if it was across the room. "She has yet to demonstrate the qualities of a future queen."

Mrs. Heifitz was once a quiet woman, but over the years, students had begun to use the school library (renamed the media room) less and less frequently. These days, there was at most a student or two—and often none at all—in the library at any given time. And so, as the years passed, Mrs. Heifitz evolved into a loud-mouthed gossip. She took the opportunity that her increasing privacy offered to gab away with her friends and fellow members of the local chapter of the Red Hat Society—a group that, as far as Jay could tell, assembled for the sole purpose of wearing red hats.

"Martha, she was wearing a purple sweater! Under

fifty years old, you are required to wear *lavender* attire! Unacceptable."

Jay looked over at her, hoping she'd get the hint to quiet down. Her clothes were as loud as her voice—a bright red hat; huge, red-rimmed glasses; and a massive purple sweater bulleted with at least a dozen pins that said things like, "Age is a State of Mind," "Fun First," and "Optimism!" Unfortunately, she didn't get the hint, and instead launched into a detailed explanation of where lavender ended and purple began. Jay longed for the city library. His mind started to wander: *Where were the librarians now? Did Professor Penfield and Miss DeHart get the books to a safe a location? Did Dr. Grunspan find Pross's boss? When would they return?*

After an hour on the computer produced no results, Jay wandered the bookshelves, grabbing any title he thought might shed some light on the symbol. He browsed through books about symbology, art history, the molecular models of compounds—even a catalog of old baseball-team logos.

Two hours later—he had now missed three classes— he was standing, bleary-eyed, in the geography aisle when he spotted a spine on the top shelf emblazoned with the title *Flags of the World*. He took down the book and found himself suddenly staring into a pair of sinister eyes.

"Hello, Jay Winnick."

"Uh—"

"Why aren't you in class, young man?" the voice asked.

"Well, you see, Mr. Fahrner…"

Vice Principal Fahrner wore a very serious look on his

face, which wasn't surprising, since this was the only sort of look he ever displayed. He had dozens of shades of serious, however, and this was one of the more severe.

Jay smiled politely and continued, "I'm looking for a book for the teacher."

"And exactly what class do you have right now?"

"Math… with Mrs. McQueen."

"And she wants you to get a book in the geography section?"

"Yep," Jay said sheepishly. "It's—it's about the different number systems across the world. Did you know that the Romans had no number for zero?"

"I think you should be returning to class now," Mr. Fahrner said, glaring through the slot in the shelf.

"But—"

"Now!"

"Can you all please keep it down?" Mrs. Heifitz hollered from her desk. "I mean, *honestly!*"


Jay sat staring at a doodle of the symbol while Mrs. McQueen droned on about the rules of multiplying fractions. Even if he didn't have a mysterious symbol to decode, his mind would have wandered away, as it always did when subjected to Mrs. McQueen.

"Multiply the numerator first," she said, her voice as lifeless as any ghost Jay had ever encountered, "and then multiply the denominator."

Jay fixed his eyes on his paper, pencil in hand,

pretending to take notes. What could it be? A punctuation mark? An Egyptian hieroglyph? He tried to think back to the book about the mummies.

"Excuse me, Mrs. McQueen, may I please see Jay Winnick?" Jay turned to see that Mr. Kachowski had popped his humongous head in the doorway.

Confused, he followed Mr. K as he waddled down the hall to the art room. There was no art class this period, but three students sat at the front table: Pam, Brian, and Danni had been plucked from their classes as well.

"What's going on?" Jay asked.

"I should ask you the same question," Mr. K said, stroking his beard and wedging himself into a seat next to the students. "Today in class, I asked everyone to draw using pastels. I received pictures of sunsets, mountains, beaches. And then I received this from Pam." He held up a pastel drawing of the crop circle symbol. Its accuracy and detail were startling. The shading was perfect, and she had managed to get the light just right.

"And this, from Danni." He held up a simpler version of the symbol. "Her pictures always depict bloodshed or some sort of grotesque scenario, so I found this one odd."

"Then I got this from Brian." Mr. K held up a horribly scribbled mess. "With some effort, I recognized this as an attempt to draw the same symbol. If you were in the same art class as these three, I am sure you would have drawn the same thing. What's going on?"

They all looked at each other, unsure what to say.

"We—we thought you might know what the symbol is," Pam admitted. "You know, from all your…" She looked up at the top shelves. "…travels."

"It's to get to the next level of the game," Brian said, scratching his ear.

"The game?" Mr. K pushed his glasses up his bulbous nose. "Your LARPing—is that what you called it?"

"Yeah," Brian said. "Live-Action Role Playing."

"It's educational," Pam said.

"And nonviolent," Danni added.

Jay looked at his friends. Maybe they weren't going with him on the quest, but they were still trying to pitch in. He smiled, while Mr. K's face grew pensive.

"Reminds me a little of the runes of ancient South American civilizations," Mr. K said thoughtfully. He shuffled the sketches. "Possibly Incan. Maybe pre-Incan…"

The bell rang, signaling the end of the period.

"Well," Mr. K said, his glance still lingering on the drawings, "I suppose you should get to your next class."

He handed Jay the sketches, and as Jay took hold of them, Mr. K's fat fingers seemed just a little reluctant to let them go.

Once the four were a safe distance from the art room, they stopped and huddled together in the hallway.

"Thanks," Jay said, looking down at Brian's drawing—the symbol was hardly recognizable. "I can really use help behind the scenes. I haven't been able to turn up anything. I've looked—"

"What are you talking about?" Pam said, sounding irritated.

Jay looked up from Brian's sketch, confused. "I thought this meant you were helping."

"We are," Pam replied. Now Jay was completely perplexed. "But we're not staying *behind the scenes*," she continued.

"Yeah," Danni said in the same irritated tone. "Do you really think I'm going to let you explore a crypt at the Cliffs of Death without me?"

Pam looked at Jay, her poker face turning to a slim, sincere smile. "We're your friends," she said, the sarcasm completely gone from her voice. "And friends are there for you when it matters most. No matter what."

"No," Brian said resolutely. "We're more than friends. We're family."

"And there's nothing more important than family," Danni added, winking at Jay.

They stood together, silent for a moment, in the pale light of the hallway. Jay's chest tightened. His teeth hurt…

The bell rang, and they hurried to class.

Mr. Linkins's hair fluttered toward the ceiling in a dazzling display. Had Jay not been staring at Pam's drawing of the symbol, the sight would have reminded him of Dr. Grunspan's wild wisps. The rest of the class, however, was fully enraptured by the experiment.

Mr. Linkins nearly shouted to be heard over the hum of

the machine. "THE VAN DE GRAAFF GENERATOR IS POWERED BY AN ELECTRIC MOTOR." His hands rested against the large silver ball that was mounted on a pedestal before him. "THE MOTOR CREATES A CONTINUOUS BUILDUP OF CHARGES. THE HUMAN BODY, AN IDEAL CONDUCTOR OF ELECTRICITY, ALLOWS THE CHARGES TO TRAVEL UP TO MY HAIR."

The bell sounded and students sighed. "Aw, man!" Thomas Roberge said as Mr. Linkins shut down the machine. "Is school over already?"

Thomas and his fellow classmates reluctantly stood up from their desks and trudged out of the room, many of them mumbling about wanting a chance to touch the generator. Jay, on the other hand, was so lost in thought that he hadn't even heard the bell. Next to the drawing, his history book was open to the section on Incan culture.

"Another mesmerizing blank piece of paper?" Mr. Linkins asked.

"Um, no," Jay said, looking up to find Mr. Linkins's hair still half-charged and confused like ruffled eagle feathers. "Just some designs. More nonsense mystical stuff."

"I've seen this symbol before."

"*You have?*" Jay could barely contain himself. "Is it Incan?"

"Incan?" Mr. Linkins looked confused. "No, I saw it in *National Skeptic* magazine. It's the symbol of some crackpot, Satellite Sam Milwit." He patted his hair back into place.

"Where'd you see this symbol?" Mr. Linkins asked.

"The crop circle," Jay said.

"That's some pretty strange viral marketing," Mr. Linkins replied, arching his eyebrow.

"So you've heard of this Satellite guy?"

"Unfortunately, yes. He's what they call a channeler."

"You mean, like, someone who is possessed by different people?

"Sort of. Supposedly, a channeler like Satellite can connect with spirits and have them speak through him." Mr. Linkins let out a pointed laugh. "Skeptics have been trying to debunk him for years."

"Why do they call him Satellite?'

"Two reasons. For one thing, because he's out there, really out there. And second…"

"Yeah?"

Mr. Linkins just chuckled softly. "No respectable skeptic would even mention it."

## CHAPTER SIXTEEN

# CHANNEL SURFING

"Are you sure this is it?" Pam asked as they approached a duplex town house with newly painted aluminum siding and brown-shuttered windows.

"It's the right address," Jay said, looking down at the Google map he had printed out. A quick search for Satellite Sam Milwit had turned up a simple website with an address and a digital version of the symbol from the crop circle.

They stepped through a well-tended lawn onto the front steps. Before the door lay a green doormat that read "Welcome Visitors." Next to it, the same mysterious symbol had been neatly painted.

"It just seems so... *ordinary*," Jay said. "I thought it'd be some creepy old house, with bats and broken shutters and spiderwebs on the windows." He pressed the doorbell, expecting—kind of hoping even—for an ominous tone, but instead it merely ding-donged like any other.

"One minute," a smooth, cordial voice said from behind the door.

It opened, and a thin, kindly looking man stood before them, smiling politely. He wore a sweater jacket along with neatly pressed khakis. His hair was tidy and his chin was sharp, with a cleft. "Can I help you?" he asked.

"Uh, hi," Jay stammered. "Sorry for just showing up like this, but we were… um… referred to you. We didn't have a number, so we just came by."

"I'm sorry, referred to me for what service?"

"You are a channeler, right?"

"Oh. Yes, sure. I also make birdhouses, so I wasn't sure which you meant." Satellite waved his hand invitingly and said, "Please come on in."

They followed him into the duplex. "So who referred you?" he asked them.

Jay wasn't exactly sure what Satellite knew about the Association or the glass, so he thought the safest thing to do was stay vague. "Uh… a client of yours."

Pam, noticing a skeptical look on Satellite's face, chimed in with her favorite fortune-telling tactic. "Dah…" She watched Satellite's face for a sign of recognition. "Dah-ar… eeeyay…" Nothing. "Dayyyy?"

"Dave?" Satellite asked.

"Yep." Pam nodded. "Good old Dave."

"Dave Greenbaum?"

"Davey G. That's him," Pam said with fake affection.

"Nice guy," Satellite smiled. "Hard to believe he wanted

to contact his grandma's spirit just to get her matzo ball soup recipe. But hey, to each his own." He waved them into the foyer, past a hat rack and some tastefully framed portrait photographs.

Jay peered around the corner and caught a glimpse of Satellite straightening stacks of papers on a dining room table covered with a vinyl tablecloth. He then grabbed a glass and something else—it looked like maybe a hand towel that had seen better days—and hurried to the kitchen.

"Anyone else freaked out by how normal this guy is?" Jay whispered. "I thought channelers and mediums and psychic types are all supposed to be nutjobs."

*"Hey,"* Pam said, "I'm standing right here."

"Sorry about that," Satellite said, hurrying back into the foyer.

"So do you think you can help us?" Jay asked.

"You're in luck. I have a free slot right now. I had a cancellation. There was a last-minute hockey practice."

"Somebody skipped the chance to contact a spirit because of hockey practice?" Danni said incredulously.

"No, it was the spirit who had practice. Enough people have died falling through the ice at Black Lake for a full hockey game. Evidently, their goalie is having difficulty staying solid as an apparition, and shots have been literally going right through him. So you see, they need the practice, of course."

"Of course," Danni replied.

"So, um, how much is it for the session?" Pam asked.

"Oh, don't worry about that." He looked at Pam and a glint of recognition registered on his face. "You're Momma Petrucci's daughter, aren't you?"

"Um, yes."

"Well, no wonder you asked how much." He chuckled to himself. "Haven't seen Momma for a while. We had a spoon-bending contest a few years back: two minutes to bend as many spoons as you could with nothing but your mind. She beat me by six spoons." Satellite smiled warmly. "Just one more second—let me tidy up the living room. It's a bit of a mess." He ducked around the wall, out of sight.

"Okay, come on in," Satellite called from the living room after a few minutes. "I've cleaned up as much as I can on such short notice."

"Well, that's an interesting look," Pam said as they entered the large, open room. All of the furniture was covered in tight, clear plastic. Not just the chairs and sofas, but also the end tables, coffee tables, bookshelves, lamps, everything. It all had a layer of shiny, translucent skin.

"We spoke too soon," Danni whispered to Jay. She rubbed her hand over a plastic-covered armchair. "This guy *is* a nutjob—must be a major germophobe."

"Make yourseves comfortable," Satellite said, gesturing to the room's chairs and sofas. He himself sat down in a dark-wood rocking chair, which, like everything else, was covered in plastic.

It was difficult to truly get comfortable on the slippery

coverings. Squeaks and scrapes and fartlike sounds made an awkward silence less silent and more awkward as they tried to settle in, their butts rubbing noisily against the taut plastic.

"*Psst.*" Danni elbowed Jay's arm to get his attention and nudged her chin toward a small table by the rocking chair.

On the table, next to a stack of books and a coffee mug that said "World's Greatest Medium," was a human skull.

"That's the same one I saw in the crystal ball," Danni said. "I can tell by the cracks."

"I see you're admiring my paperweight," Satellite said to her. He picked up the skull. "A gift from a client. He thought it was funny—because of the whole speaking-to-the-dead thing. I find it a bit morbid, of course, but it's impolite to refuse a gift." He set the skull back down. "He comes by every now and then, so if I didn't display it, I'd never hear the end of it."

The plastic wasn't the only thing peculiar about the furniture. It was arranged so that every chair and sofa was angled to face the same area of the room. But the point of focus wasn't a TV or fireplace—instead, the furniture was all turned toward the rocking chair in which Satellite now sat, rocking gently.

"The guide and the remote are on the coffee table," he said.

Sure enough, on the table, next to a journal titled *Spirit-Induced Automatic Writing*, was a clipboard on which

# Spirit Guide

*"History in the palm of your hand"*™

| Frequency | Name of Spirit | Cause of Death |
|-----------|----------------|----------------|
| 97.5 | Charles Jones | Bubonic plague (1352) |
| 98.1 | Paul Perry | Public hanging (1685) |
| 98.6 | Gregory Sturm | Hunting "accident" (1874) |
| 98.9 | Simon Morgan | Crash-induced depression (1931) |
| 99.6 | Takahashi Horito | Kamikaze (1941) |
| 99.9 | Ken Klyne | Smoking-related illness (1957) |
| 100.1 | Elvis Presley | Cardiac arrhythmia (1977) |
| 100.3 | Murray Edelson | Freak disco ball mishap (1978) |
| 100.5 | Milt Thomas, radio star | Video (1983) |
| 100.7 | Joey "Lucky" Grimaldi | Shot to death (1986) |
| 101.2 | Jenteal Levinique | Shock (1990) |
| 102.6 | Larry Mickleballs | Natural causes/iron to face (1995) |
| 104.8 | Jeff Sank | Laughed to death (2004) |

**Rules and Regulations:**

• Any rebroadcast or retransmission of the Spirit Medium's utterances, communications, or ramblings is strictly forbidden without the express ghostwritten consent of the respective spirit.

• Spirit Medium cannot be held liable for guarantees, assertions, or slander made by a channeled spirit. Any litigation must be pursued exclusively against the spirit's estate.

• Regarding automated writings, Spirit Medium retains, exclusively, irrevocably, perpetually, and throughout the universe, all right, title, and interest, including the worldwide copyright (and any registrations and applications relating thereto and any renewals and extensions thereof).

• As a courtesy, during a trance state, please do not touch, injure, or otherwise physically accost Spirit Medium. Similarly, do not rob his house, consume his food, or dress him up in funny outfits for amusement.

*—Thanks from "all of us"!*

was clamped a laminated piece of paper titled "Spirit Guide."

"Does anyone want something to eat or drink?" Satellite asked. "Rude of me not to offer."

"No, thanks," Jay said as he tried to make sense of the laminated paper. The chart featured a grid with a column of numbers. A second column was full of names that corresponded to the numbers, while a third column listed the cause of death for each name.

Next to the clipboard was a square brown box with a small knob and a digital readout window. The box was homemade, with wires connected to several exposed circuit boards.

Seeing the puzzled look on Jay's face, Satellite launched into an explanation. "The trance is based on electrical charges and electromagnetic frequencies. You use that dial to tune me into various spirits." He pointed to the box. "Isn't technology amazing?" he said gleefully. "We're working on an app next."

Jay studied the chart. As he scanned the names, he thought about the latest riddle: "Now that you have seen your sign... Take a visit back in time... Find your voice to set you free... And lead you to the special key."

Jay looked up from the chart. "So this is basically like a *TV Guide* of the different spirits you can connect with?"

"I am, after all, a *channeler*," Satellite smiled, rocking steadily. "It's more like a radio dial of frequencies. Once I am in a trance state, tune to one of the numbers and you'll find yourself communicating with the respective spirit. If you don't like it, change the channel using the dial. I won't be offended."

Jay ran his thumb down the paper. "So we may have to go through all of these to get what we want?"

"Not if you know that one of those spirits on the paper has your answer."

Jay skimmed the chart. He didn't recognize any of the names or have any reason to believe that one of them knew anything about the key.

"Those are only the known channels," Satellite pointed out. "The ones that consistently come in. As you turn the dial, other spirits might come through on different frequencies. Now, if you don't mind, we need to get started. I have a three p.m. with a woman who is looking to connect with her dead cousin to ask permission to date her widowed husband. Can you believe that? But who am I to judge?"

Satellite reached down behind his chair and picked up a metal object. It was flat, with three short prongs extending downward and a strap hanging from it—like an armor helmet that had been crushed in a vise.

"What's that?" Danni asked curiously.

"My antenna," he said as he placed the object on his head. "It helps with reception." He snapped the strap across his chin. "Yet another miracle of technology."

Brian chuckled.

"Something funny?" Satellite asked him.

"No, I—I just have a metal hat too."

As Satellite adjusted his antenna, Pam suddenly realized what the symbol meant. It was a stick-figure representation of the medium wearing his "antenna."

"Just give me a minute to get into a trance." Satellite tilted his head back and closed his eyes. All of a sudden, he began to convulse spastically as if he was being shocked with jumper cables. His head jerked from side to side, and strange words began to spout from his mouth: "Lababjabbajja... Bbjaabjab... Babklogojogo... Mogoozip... Zzipzipa... Cahcahahhhhhhhhh..." His head fell forward and he was silent. He opened his eyes and stared at the floor. The look on his face was beyond blank; it was lifeless, like a wax sculpture.

"He's in," Pam said. "Turn on the dial."

Jay turned the knob on the remote and it clicked. As he turned the dial, a high-pitched squeal that sounded like microphone feedback emanated from Satellite's mouth. The feedback faded and more nonsense words gushed forth: "Klokodockybahbah... Siswakanahndy... Sheepadeepdope..." Occasionally a recognizable word fizzled in and out of the gibberish.

Turning the dial was like surfing the radio trying to find a clear signal, and the speaking in tongues was like the static between stations. A small digital display showed the frequency like on a car radio.

Jay tuned to one of the stations listed on the chart: 100.7; *Joey "Lucky" Grimaldi; shot to death (1986)*. Satellite suddenly sprung to life—it was like putting a quarter into an animatronic mascot at Chuck E. Cheese's. His hands moved wildly as he talked, and he spoke with a heavy New York Italian accent.

"…outta nowhere, so I can't say fuh sure who did it. All I know is dat I feel sumpin' smack duh backa my head twice. Like, *bam-bam*, y'know? Next ding I know, I'm in duh trunk of a Buick. It was Sal 'Duh Duck' Deluca's car. I know dat smell anywhere. So dey pull me out, right— bag over my head—and I hear, 'Don't mess with duh Nacarato family,' and den I hear a gunshot. Next ding I know—*boom!*—I'm at duh bottom of duh ocean or river or sumpin.' But somehow I can breathe. And dat's when it hits me: I'm a ghost, stuck underwater. Dat's why I'll dake any chance I can get with a medium, because otherwise my entire social circle has gills, y'know what I'm sayin'?"

Pam, growing impatient, interrupted the rant. "Do you know where the Dominion Glass key is?"

"Key? What key? I don't know nuttin' about nuttin'. I'm innocent."

"Change the channel, Jay," Pam said, and then she turned toward Satellite. "Sorry, Joey, time to sleep with the fishes. Bye now."

Jay turned the dial to 101.2 (*Jenteal Levinique; died of shock in 1990 upon seeing an outfit that she described—in her own bubbly ghostwriting, no less—"as if a peacock had turned itself inside out"*). Satellite's posture completely changed. He crossed his legs, wiped his hair behind his ears, and leaned forward. He smacked his lips and his speech became high-pitched, fast, and, most startlingly, female. Words raced forth with hardly a breath between them.

"…and that is a definite no-no, mmmkay? You thought the living had fashion problems; you would not believe what the lifeless—and clueless, can I just say—here in the spirit realm are wearing. I mean, total horror stories. Nightmares among nightshades. I always thought I'd see chic, flowing white robes or something timeless, death being eternal and all, but instead, it's more bridesmaid than bride. I am forced to look at every fashion faux pas in history: ill-fitting codpieces, unflattering monk frocks, baggy flannels. In my fashion column, I used to say that I wouldn't be caught dead wearing polyester. Let me just say, I wish others would have made the same pact. And then there are the cursed ones, those forced to carry chains. I mean, I'm all for a little bling, but two hundred pounds of steel shackles? *Puh-lease!* Oh, and being transparent does not hide weight issues at all. It just makes all the bad parts easier to see."

"Should we even bother?" Danni asked.

Jay shrugged and gave it a shot: "We're looking to find the key to the Dominion Glass. It's a crystal."

"Crystal?" the voice snorted. "Not interested. Talk to me if you're looking for actual diamonds."

Jay fiddled with the box's knob. The next frequency wasn't until 102.6, but he turned the knob slowly. A voice fought with the spirit static, so Jay stopped. "*Me llamo Pedro.*

*Uno pregunta: Donde esta el baño en el mundo del muerte?"*

"Anyone speak Spanish?" Jay asked. They all shook their heads, so he turned the dial again, toward the next designated station. Another voice broke through the static. At first there were just half words and blips of sounds, but somehow the voice sounded familiar, so Jay tuned the dial delicately until he could hear it. The voice was quiet but clear enough: "Son… is that you?"

# CHAPTER SEVENTEEN

## A VOICE FROM THE PAST

J ay leaned forward and desperately tried to tweak the dial to get better reception.

"Son?"

He crept toward Satellite's chair. The channeler's body was still, calm, his arms at his sides as if stuck.

"Jay?"

"Dad… it's me, Jay."

No answer.

"Can you hear me? Dad, is it you?"

At that moment, something odd happened. Satellite's eyes blinked—it was the first time they had done so since the trance started—and when he opened them, they were no longer brown. They were sharp blue.

"Dad?"

The nonsensical static got louder. It seemed like two stations were battling to come in: one transmitting unintelligible jabbering, and the other picking up the faintly audible but recognizable voice of Jay's father, Michael Winnick. Jay could barely hear the next words: "In the… *zappadingadah*… coming… *bengabroffahn*… forgotten… *glicky-glicky*… you… *nyehnyehnvamamumu*… someone… *lelanikai*… close… *dadasmoof*… betray… *refwoofaydalah*… *genyennaommmmmmmmmmmm*…"

Then there was nothing but the warbling static of unrecognizable ramblings. Jay turned the knob a little to the left, then a little to the right. He tilted the box at every angle he could. He walked around the room as if he was trying to find reception on a cell phone. But all he got was spirit static and clips of the people listed on the chart. He approached Satellite and started to reach toward him.

Pam yelled out, "Jay, no!"

"Maybe I need to adjust the angle of his head."

"You can't touch him. You'll break his trance. And we still need info about the key."

"She's right, Jay," Danni agreed. "This may be our only chance."

"Just give me more time."

"You're not thinking clearly, Jay," Pam said, getting up and walking over to him. She reached toward the box. He tried to push her hands away, which caused him to accidentally turn the dial.

Satellite fell quiet. He blinked and his eyes were brown again. He sat silent for a moment and then pulled his legs up into the chair and sat Indian-style. He rested his wrists on his knees and touched his pinkies to his thumbs. He took three slow breaths and said, "Seek the key, do we?" The voice was soft and crackled with age, tinged with a strange accent—southeastern Chinese, Danni thought. "The key to the glass?"

"Yes, the key to the Dominion Glass," Brian said quickly.

The voice stayed perfectly peaceful. "Why do you seek the key to the glass?"

Brian looked to Jay, expecting him to speak, but Jay sat on the plastic-covered ottoman, frozen and silent, as if in his own trance.

Pam moved in toward Satellite, next to Brian. She looked into Satellite's eyes, but it was like looking at windows with the blinds pulled down. "Who are we speaking with?" she asked. "Do you have the key?"

Satellite smiled lightly. "I had the key you speak of, but it has been passed on. Why seek such a dangerous thing when there are flowers to be gathered and raindrops to let fall on one's tongue?"

"Just our luck," Brian said. "Our spirit is a flake."

"Brian, quiet!" Pam ordered. She spoke in a calm, steady tone. "We want to keep it safe."

"I sense that not all of you are in agreement about what to do with the glass," the spirit said.

Satellite turned his head toward Jay, who was looking at the Spirit Guide list. Jay looked up, caught the again-brown eyes of Satellite, looked at his friends, and then quickly back down at the paper.

"We want to protect the glass," Pam explained. "From people—"

The voice interrupted her. "I care little for words. They are like clouds blocking my view of the moonlight." Satellite lifted his hands and opened his palms. He closed his eyes. "Please. Be silent. Be still."

Satellite turned his head again toward Jay, who looked up from the channel listing at the medium. His eyes were closed, but Jay felt like Satellite (or whoever he was at the moment) was looking right at him. When Satellite turned away, Jay felt like a weight had been lifted from him.

The old voice finally spoke again: "To find the key… you must see my student, a teacher. You must be found by being deserted."

"Somebody write this down," Pam said, desperately searching her pockets for a pen.

"Got it," Brian said, taking a puzzle book and mechanical pencil from his back pocket. He began scribbling in the margin as Satellite continued his riddles.

"You must go where up is down and down is up. Follow the stream to its end, which is its beginning. There you shall lose everything and find the key."

After a few moments, it became clear that the riddles had stopped. Pam cleared her throat. "Is that all, sir?

"One more thing," he answered. "You must take me with you."

"B-b-but," Pam stammered. "How can we…? Do you mean take Satellite?"

"No. I shall make myself manifest in the physical world."

That's when things got very weird. And very disgusting.

A pale, gooey slime began spewing out of Satellite's left nostril.

"What the…?" Brian gasped.

"Nasty!" Pam said.

"Awesome!" Danni gushed.

More goo dripped out of both his ears, like melting earwax, until it flowed and connected into the jellied mass slobbering from out of Satellite's lower lip. His mouth parted and more of the secretion oozed and bubbled into the blob that was beginning to resemble pancake batter baking into a solid circle.

"It's like a super booger," Pam said, wide-eyed with shock.

"That booger is taking some kind of shape," Brian said, disgusted by the slimy mass that now extended past Satellite's chin like a beard.

"Ectoplasm," Pam explained. "It's the spirit taking physical form."

Sure enough, seconds later a gelatinous mass hung from the medium's nose and mouth, forming an unmistakable shape. Satellite had just sneezed out a face. It looked like a slimy latex mask.

Brian began gagging violently in the corner, making deep guttural sounds very similar to Satellite's earlier jabbering. And though Pam had heard Momma speak of spiritual ectoplasm many times, she had never actually seen it before. She too had to turn away in disgust. Danni, however, cheerfully approached Satellite, grabbed the hanging face, and tugged. A long, slimy strand stretched like taffy until finally it snapped, and Danni held the face in her hands. She raised it in front of Pam, who jerked her head away. "So, Pam," she said, "this is the face of the spirit who was just speaking, right?"

Pam nodded, pinching her nose. "Not the actual face," she said in a nasally voice. "But it represents the spirit, yes."

"I know it's not the actual face. Duh." Danni turned the slimy ivory-white face toward her own. "Although the detail is amazing."

"Now I see why he covers his furniture," Brian gagged, still turned away from Satellite.

"Hope you found what you were looking for," Satellite said, rising from his rocker. His voice, facial expression, and posture were his own again.

He was just as they had met him, aside from the gallons of gross goo that still exuded from the orifices of his face like a pasta maker's uncooked noodles. Some of it had pooled on his chair, while a loose strand coiled on the coffee table.

"I hate to be impolite," Satellite apologized, pulling the gook from his nose and ears. "But as you can see, I need to clean up for my next appointment. Look at me."

He grabbed a hanging strand of ectoplasm from his left ear. "I am such a mess."

As he saw them out the front door, he gave a friendly wave. "Bye now," he said. "Have a nice day."

When Danni stepped down onto the doormat, she had a whole new appreciation for its message.

# CHAPTER EIGHTEEN

# AN INVITATION

As they walked back to the bus stop, Jay started to come out of his cocoon of silence. "It was him," he said to Pam. "Not just his writing or an orb of light. That was his voice."

"We can go back," she said. "We can go back and try to tune into your father."

"Who knows if we can find the signal again?"

"Jay, he's finding ways to get to you: the dreams, now this. It's a good sign."

As happy and moved as Jay was to hear his father, he wasn't sure if "good sign" was the right term. Amid the static of Satellite's tongue-speak, he distinctly heard the words "someone," "close," and "betray." He looked at his three best friends. *No way,* he thought. *They wouldn't.*

His dad was warning him about something. That much seemed clear. Still, Jay's best bet at getting to the bottom of it, of actually getting to his dad, was to get to the glass.

So when they hopped on the bus to take them back home, he joined the others as they tried to decipher the next clue. There was only one other person on the bus, an old man sitting up front, so the kids clustered in the very back as Jay read the next poem/riddle in *The Dominion Glass*:

*When you've found your souvenir*
*Take it to the one true seer*
*In its stead, he will give*
*Something dead that still lives*
*With it, you shall find your way*
*But only by the light of day.*

"The souvenir has to be the face," Jay said confidently.

"But where do we take it?" Pam asked, looking down at the poem. "Who's the one true seer?"

Brian, meanwhile, stared down at the puzzle book where he had jotted down the five sentences that the spirit had spoken. The only one whose face wasn't buried in a book was Danni—not counting the bodiless face of ectoplasm. Still in good spirits from the disgusting show they had all just witnessed, Danni held the flaccid face in front of her own and imitated Satellite's last voice as she moved the mask's mouth. "Let us be tickled by the breeze and hold dewdrops in our hands," she rasped.

The lone bus patron cast a curious glance back at them, and Danni quickly dropped the face into her lap.

"I can't crack 'em," Brian said, pinkie again racing

across his eyebrow. "The sentences contradict themselves." He shook his head in frustration as he read aloud from his notes. "'You must see my student, a teacher. You must be found by being deserted. You must go where up is down and down is up.' It's all flaky mysticism." He threw down his pencil. "Plus, it doesn't seem to have anything to do with the riddle in the book." He looked over to Jay. "Do you have any idea about this?"

"No," Jay said, stuffing *The Dominion Glass* into his backpack. "But I know someone who might."

Brian immediately understood. "Right. Why don't you sleep on it?"

**XL259:**
Whjat is the updatre?v
**GeeKing:**
SYMBOL=MEDIUM
**XL259:**
Have tghe cjhildren see him
**GeeKing:**
NS
**XL259:**
What does that mean?
**GeeKing:**
Not sure
**XL259:**
Then don't typre it, We need to do sometihing

**GeeKing:**
> WUT DO U WANT 2 DO

**XL259:**
> I have an idea.

That night, Jay pressed RECORD on his digital recorder and placed it on his nightstand. Then he opened *The Dominion Glass* and put the pneumaticles on top. He felt like a kid hoping for a visit from the tooth fairy—desperate to fall asleep, which of course made doing so almost impossible. Finally, after a few hours, he managed to doze off....

Suddenly, he was at the water park and, once again, everything was going backward. This time, he stood outside of the pool, using a wet towel to slather water all over his body. He rubbed the towel over his head, soaking his hair and matting it down on his skull. He tossed the now-dry towel to a lifeguard, who caught it and said, *"Seird ti erom eht rettew steg ti."* Jay hurled himself backward into the pool. The splash was swallowed; he was yanked back onto the slide and reeled back up to the top, where his father caught him with open arms.

In a flash of sunlight, Jay was transported to a parking lot. His father was nowhere in sight. Oddly, instead of cars, the parking lot was full of camels. Jay wandered past the chewing beasts, looking for his father. "Dad!" he called out. *"Dad...?"*

When Jay awoke, he immediately fumbled through the

pictures on his nightstand for the pneumaticles. He put the glasses on and looked down at *The Dominion Glass*. Nothing.

He scanned the page, making sure he wasn't missing anything. He took the glasses off, breathed on the lenses, and wiped them with his shirt. Still nothing. Weird. His dad was in his dream. Not for long, but it should have been long enough for him to have written a word or two. And so Jay's unsettled mood lifted little as he went downstairs to start his day with the unappealing ritual of his wicker cereal and tomato juice.

Danni and Pam were waiting for Jay when he approached his locker that morning.

"Anything?" Danni asked.

"No," he said. "I dreamed about him, but no note."

"We should still hit the music room after school to check for EVP," she said.

"Yeah," Jay agreed.

"What was the dream?" Pam asked.

"What does it matter?"

"Momma's making me study dream interpretation. It could be a premonition."

"A what?"

"A premonition," Brian said as he approached. "A warning of things to come." He leaned into Jay. "If anyone cool comes by, just pretend I'm asking to copy your homework."

"Whatever," Jay said.

"Pathetic," Pam added. Then she turned to Jay and said, "Your dream could be trying to tell us something."

"It was the water-park dream again."

"Water can mean lots of things: rebirth, danger, change—"

She was interrupted by a smattering of high-pitched giggles. A group of Genevra's friends had just rounded the corner and were closing in like a swarm of buzzing gnats. As they approached, Brian quickly turned to Pam and grunted, "So you got that vocab list done for me, right?"

Pam looked at Brian impatiently and then cleared her throat deliberately. "Why, yes, I do." She spoke as if acting in a Shakespearean play. "I shall give it to you right away, kind sir."

The girls all turned their heads toward Pam and held their glances just long enough to make it clear they weren't interested in her. They then looked to Brian and smiled in perfect sync. As quickly as they had come, they flittered away, their giggles fading into the general noise in the halls.

"What was that?" Brian asked Pam, irritated.

"Acting," Pam replied with a smile.

"We needed that hint from your dad, Jay," Danni said, returning to the task at hand. "Hopefully, we'll hear something on the recording. Or else we're stuck."

"Maybe you should take a nap," Pam suggested.

"I do have Mrs. McQueen fourth period," Jay said, opening his locker door.

A piece of paper fell out. It was blank.

"How long does this LARPing game last?" Mr. Kachowski asked, his mouth full of chocolaty nougat. He was retouching the paint on an elaborately carved wooden tribal mask, and it seemed to be taking a fair amount of concentration.

"It's kind of ongoing," Brian said quickly, scratching his cheek.

Danni looked at him and shook her head; she really needed to coach him to lie in a more natural way.

Mr. K used the end of his paintbrush to pick some nougat from the roof of his mouth. "Go ahead," he grumbled, licking a clump of brown off the edge of the brush. "The kiln is all yours."

For the third time, the heat from the kiln revealed the lemon-juice writing.

"What do they mean, 'the rumors about the cave'?" Brian asked, stealing a glance at Mr. K, who was still busy with the mask—and his fourth Snickers.

"They say Dragon Teeth Cave is haunted," Jay said.

"Well, then," Pam said snappily, "seems like a splendid place to meet."

"Actually, it makes sense," Jay said, lowering his voice. "The Association comes up with something superscary to keep the place private."

"I don't know," Pam said, staring down at the letter. "Something doesn't feel right to me."

"Something always doesn't feel right to you," Brian

shot back. "Breakfast doesn't feel right to you."

Pam's first instinct was to say, "You try eating pancakes on a spirit board!" But instead, she looked squarely at Brian and pouted, "*You* don't feel right to me."

"Good one." Brian shook his head and let out a superior sigh.

"You know," Mr. K rumbled as he swept a flourish of green paint across the mask, "many cultures considered caves to be the domain of the haunted." He swallowed the cud of candy in his mouth, then continued, "The ancient Greeks believed that spirits escaped from the underworld through cracks and fissures in the stone and into the caves above."

He gazed up at them dreamily and pulled at the fringes of his beard. Then he looked at his fingers, smelled them, and, realizing that he had groomed some chocolate free from his beard, licked his fingers clean.

Jay reread the letter. The writing had already begun to fade. "I guess we'll have to listen to the recording tomorrow," he said. "This is more important."

This time the excuse was that they were all invited to dinner at Pam's house. Jay knew he was pressing his luck; his mom tended to call and check in on him, and it was only the awkward feeling she got when talking to Momma Petrucci that kept her from calling to make sure that he was abiding by the restrictions of his nonexistent food allergies.

As usual, Pam didn't bother lying to Momma. She just said she was going to explore a dark, mysterious cave, and Momma felt this was a suitable after-school activity.

The four of them rode their bikes to Dragon Teeth Cave, since it was a good five miles outside of town. As they veered off the main road onto the trail to the cave, Pam immediately regretted not having a mountain bike. Brian pedaled hard, skillfully weaving his way through the woods, up hills, and over tree roots. Jay and Danni followed, not nearly as fast, but managing, while Pam, on the narrow tires of her ten-speed, had to keep calling out to them to wait up.

The trail was overgrown with weeds and tree branches, and soon it was barely a trail at all, just wide enough for their bike tires to maneuver around the random rocks and fallen logs. It appeared that the rumors of the cave being haunted had accomplished exactly what the Association had intended. Nobody ventured down this trail.

As they rode deeper into the forest, the thick canopy of trees blotted out most of the remaining dusk light. It may as well have been nighttime by the time they reached the entrance to the cave. Fortunately, Jay was prepared. He reached into his backpack and pulled out four mining headlamps, small flashlights affixed to adjustable headbands. He tossed one to each of his friends.

"Just strap it on your head and then twist the light to turn it on," he explained, illuminating his own.

Only Pam had trouble following the instructions

because she couldn't figure out what to do with her bangs. If they went under the band, they were pressed in front of her eyes; over the band, and they were swept up in front of the light. Between the rocky, rooted path and this new annoyance, Pam felt that forces were at work trying to tell her to stay away from the cave. But she kept quiet, eventually pulling her bangs back and stuffing them into the sides of the headband, before reluctantly joining the others as they stared into the gaping entrance of Dragon Teeth Cave.

The opening was about six feet high and wide enough for two people to enter shoulder to shoulder.

"Looks more like a snake's mouth," Danni said, angling her head to light up the two rocky spikes hanging down like fangs over the entrance.

Even many longtime Rockville residents didn't know how Dragon Teeth Cave really got its name. Most people mistakenly believed it was named for the dinosaur fossils (including teeth) that had been found there; however, the cave actually got its name, as Jay explained, from its many sharp stalactites, which tapered to sharp points like a dragon's teeth.

"Which one is a stalactite and which is a stalagmite?" Danni asked.

"Stalactites hang from the roof," Brian answered. "They hang on *tight*. That's how you can remember it."

Jay stepped into the cave, his headlamp shining in the darkness like the giant eye of a Cyclops. Danni and Brian followed, with Pam straggling in behind them, looking nervously back over her shoulder toward the forest. The beam from her headlamp slashed through the trees. At least nothing was following them—as far as she could tell.

"Are there stalagmites too?" Danni said. "I mean, if it's supposed to resemble a dragon's mouth or whatever, there should be some bottom teeth."

As their headlamps lit up the cave, Danni realized she was wrong. There weren't any stalagmites. Instead, on the cave's floor, as still as the rocks above, was a crystal pool. In the glow of the light beams, the lake perfectly reflected the sharp stalactites above, giving the feeling of being inside the jaws of some massive dragon.

Jay turned his head, shining light into the cavern's corners. The pool filled up the entire chamber. "Dr. Grunspan?" Jay's call railed against the rocky walls. "Professor Penfield?" There was no answer other than a pronounced echo. "It's us. We got your note."

"Maybe they're not here yet," Brian said, trying to stifle the tremor in his voice. He wasn't sure why, but the moment he stepped into the cave, he felt a strange sense of foreboding.

He wasn't the only one. Danni felt her shoulder tingle. The wound from the library ghost hadn't hurt in days, but suddenly it burned like bare skin against ice. Jay aimed his headlight over the water to the far end of the chamber. As the light fell onto a dark patch, he realized that a tunnel continued on the other side of the lake.

"I guess we have to cross the lake," he said. He dipped his foot into the pool, instinctively stepping around the illusion of spikes protruding from the floor. He half-expected to fall as he stepped into the reflected dome of the cave. Immediately, he jerked his foot out of the water and yelped.

"What's the matter?" Pam asked. "Did you step on something?"

"No, it's just… *cold*. Much colder than you'd expect." Jay braced himself and stepped back into the water. It was so cold, it seemed thick—almost solid—like he was walking through snow. "It's pretty shallow," he said as he reached the middle of the lake. The water rose just above his knees.

The others winced as they shuffled through the freezing water and joined Jay at the center of the chamber. He looked into the glossy pool and saw his own face looking back. He was just about to head to the other side when something in the water moved.

# CHAPTER NINETEEN

## FACES OF THE ENEMY

At first Jay thought it was just the light from his headlamp skirting about the surface of the pool, but no, whatever was in the water had shape to it.

It swam around his leg, and though Jay felt nothing, he nearly jumped. Strangely, the water didn't move. Not even the tiniest ripple disturbed the stalactites reflected from the cave's roof.

"Did you guys see that?" Jay asked.

Soon, all four of them were frantically jerking their heads, trying to find whatever was in the water.

"Everyone stop moving." Jay aimed his headlamp down at the water. "Just look down and stay still." A few feet in front of him, a pocket of the lake appeared to be swirling. "See that whirlpool?" He nudged his chin toward the spinning haze.

"I don't think that's a whirlpool," Brian said. "The water…" He aimed his light on top of Jay's. "…it's not moving."

Something in the water was spinning, but the water itself was perfectly still. Another circle of light suddenly swirled to life in front of Danni. Moments later, two more rings appeared between Pam and Brian.

Just as Jay leaned down to get a closer look, the ring unraveled and shot toward him in a straight line. It slithered around his legs, reforming into a ring, encircling him. In a flash, each of them was surrounded by one of the mysterious rings.

They looked down, jousting their light beams to pierce the water's surface, trying to make sense of the spinning smoke. Then, the circling blurs slowed and, like a carousel coming to a stop, the streaks of light gradually settled into shapes.

"Fish?" Jay wondered to himself. He steadied his gaze into the glimmering water and swallowed hard. This was no fish. At his feet was a twisted and tangled human form. Still, the water was as smooth as glass.

That's when Jay thought to look up.

Directly above his head, a ghostly body circled a long, dagger-sharp stalactite. Of course, the water didn't move—there was nothing in it. A reflection. For each of the four spinning swirls, a ghost orbited one of the ceiling's stalactites. Around they spun, their reflections tightening like nooses around the ghost hunters' ankles.

As with predatory animals, there are certain patterns to ghost attacks. In the library's Rare Book Room, the ghosts demonstrated the common sharklike behavior of circling their prey before they struck. Here again, it was only a matter of time.

The ghosts stopped circling and hovered in the domed chamber like flakes in a snow globe. Jay tried to look them over to gauge the era of their deaths, searching for some detail in their wardrobe that might help him in combat. To his surprise, the ghosts wore no clothes at all. They were just blue-white masses of hazy light. Strangely, they appeared to be on fire, or somehow *made* of fire. Blue flame stretched and twisted—ghosts within ghosts—clinging to the forms like a fiery cloak. Protruding from the flickering blurs were long, skeletal hands. But it was the ghosts' faces that most befuddled Jay. They were fuzzy, unfocused, and constantly changing, morphing from one visage to the next, pausing only for a moment before blurring and changing into something new.

As the ghosts plunged from the rocky ceiling, their reflections in the pool seemed to rise, making Jay feel like he was being attacked from all sides. The water stirred to life as the first ghost landed in front of him. Jay locked in on its face. It blurred and shifted, held focus for a second or two, and then fell into a blank haze until a new face took shape for just a moment before it too was lost.

Jay's breath became deep and he could feel his heart beating against his expanding chest. He clenched his jaw so hard it hurt. He'd been scared of ghosts before, but never like this. It was as if everything else fell out of focus into the darkness of the cave's fringes, and it was just him and the ghost. He could feel the familiar crease carve itself into his brow, so deep it felt like it was digging into his skull. And that's when Jay realized that he wasn't afraid at all. He was mad.

*They'd been set up! By Pross!* The thought jolted him from his shock, and, furious, he slung his backpack off his shoulder, tearing at the zipper. He jabbed his hand into the pack and pulled out a stick of sage and a match.

The sage erupted gold in the darkness of the cave. Between the sage flares, headlamps, and glowing swarm of ghosts, the cave gleamed alive like a laser show. Jay swung the sage in wild arcs, but the ghost didn't budge. The pungent smoke sifted through the ghost into the shadows of the cave's dome. The sage flames tickled into the spirit's form, intermingling with those of the ghost. To his surprise, the fire blazed as if doused with gas.

Unfazed, the ghost thrust its hand into the pool—it looked as if its bony fist was piercing the limestone roof reflected from above, and when the hand emerged from the pool, it clutched a sword. Jay immediately recognized the weapon; he had seen it in the crystal ball.

One by one, the other ghosts landed. And one by one, they plunged their hands into the pool, each pulling a weapon from its hidden depths: an ax, a scythe, a spiked mace.

Jay crouched down and, with his free hand, searched the bottom of the pool for a weapon of his own. Brian, Pam, and Danni followed his lead. All four of them fell to their hands and knees, the water soaking their bones with a bracing cold. They found nothing but mud and stone. Jay dug his hands into the wet earth, scraping away, hoping he might feel the chill of metal. He smacked the water in frustration—no, this was more than frustration. This was rage.

Next to him, Pam was feeling the same seething anger take hold of her. She had told them this was a bad idea. Nobody believed her. As usual. "You happy we came now?" she yelled at no one in particular.

"Shut up, Pam!" Brian screamed back. She was right, of course. And that just made him madder. But what was most infuriating was that he was outsmarted—plain and simple.

The ghosts fanned out. Each one zeroed in on a living counterpart, driving the ghost hunters apart. The light from Jay's headlamp was beaten back by the blue-white glow of the ghost, making it hard to see. But as he steadied his head and the lamp upon the ghost, he saw, amid the flashing faces, his third-grade teacher, Mr. Dillon—his least favorite teacher ever. His anger became tinged with a note of confusion—Mr. Dillon wasn't dead. In fact, he had told Jay to stop running in the halls two days ago.

But as quickly as the man's flashing face had come, it was gone, and the ghost's head sizzled and blinked like an old TV set changing channels, flashing other faces that Jay recognized: a mean old neighbor, a counselor from camp who always yelled at him, his great-aunt who had come to visit when he was three; (in a fit, she had thrown his toys away because they were too noisy).

Jay whirled and stabbed the sage into the ghost. The flame burned in the middle of its chest, beneath the fluttering faces, but the ghost held its ground. As Jay watched the gold flame go silver behind the veil of the ghost's body, he realized with a blink of clarity the nature of the enemy he was facing. He threw the sage into the pool, and the water swallowed its flame.

He tried to think back to what he had read about purgatory ghosts in the EP, but his mind was scrambled with rage and he could only recall a few random words. They floated alone and meaningless, the way Pam saw ghostwriting. Besides, at the moment, Jay swelled with too much feeling to have time for thought.

And then the strobing faces stopped, the shadows darkened, and one face held. Tiny chin, beady, conniving eyes, that telltale smirk: Jonathan Pross.

As a second ghost wafted toward Brian, he recognized the faces of his friends. Well, not his friends exactly. His pretend friends of his pretend self—fellow jocks, popular kids, and beautiful people.

"You're a fraud," said Rob Grimaldi, cocaptain of the soccer team. "A complete…"—the face changed to Brooke Johnson, Genevra's best, and most annoying, friend—"…and utter fraud," Brooke's voice squeaked, before its features fell into shadow, giving way to Brian's soccer coach.

Barely noticeable against Brian's growing rage was a stranger, less familiar feeling, kind of like the one he got when Danni watched him lie to Genevra. It was as if the ghost was observing him. Or searching him. That was it, as if the ghost was reaching into him and pulling things out, rustling through his mind or his—

"Hey, dork."

A new face flickered to clarity on the ghost's sloping shoulders.

Randy Mingo was just as Brian remembered him, exactly as he had last seen the boy in second grade, on that day of torment. The face was obscured in the billowing light, but it was him.

"Danni, do you see this?" Brian asked.

But Danni was preoccupied with her own attacker. The ghost's hair hung down in tendrils of light, like streaks of lightning blurring into the hairs of its beard, which glowed like candlewicks. The ghost raised the mace over its shoulder. Even as she stepped back, Danni's innocent face furrowed with a look Brian had never seen before.

Brian turned his attention back to the ghost now looming over him. It felt weird looking up into the face of a child. Then the mouth hollowed, the eyes gaped into deep, dark slots, and the face hardened into bone.

As the shrouded ghost edged forward with the massive scythe, its face now dark and hooded, Brian felt like he was staring into the face of death itself. Aware only of the fury inside himself, he took a step forward.

Across the pool, the ghost before Pam finally buzzed clear. Her jaw dropped in horror. She was staring at a mirror image of her own face, as clear and accurate as the reflection from the cave pool.

# CHAPTER TWENTY

## ONE LAST BREATH

"**Y**ou literally can't stand the sight of yourself, can you?" Pam's own voice gave her chills as it seeped from the ghost's flickering mouth. "That's okay. I can't either." Then, with a strength Pam could never hope to achieve, the ghost hoisted the battle-ax into the air.

On the other side of the pool, the light seemed to highlight Pross's stupid grin. For a moment, Jay was filled with a twisted hope—was Pross dead? Then he quickly remembered that many of the faces he was seeing weren't dead. The ghost was stealing the faces of the living, using them.

When Pross's likeness spoke, it wasn't his voice, at least not completely. His mouth moved, the face was his, but the words were borrowed from the faces Jay had just seen, clipped together unnaturally, the way a computer speaks. "I. Am. Going. To. Get. The. Glass," the mishmash of voices said. "And. Then. You'll. Never. See. Your. Father. Again. Dead. Or. Alive."

The venom coursing through Jay's veins flooded his chest and shot down his arms. He reared back, ready to lunge toward the ghost. But then Pross's features blurred. The chin rounded and the jaw squared. The forehead became broad and strong, and the eyes filled with a deep blue light.

Michael Winnick's face was clearer than what Jay had seen in the forest fog. And though it was tinged with a ghostly light, it was closer and more detailed than the best of his two and a half pictures. As the figure moved toward him, the flames flickered atop the water, and it appeared to be gliding on the surface of the pool. Jay stepped away and slipped on the slick pool floor, falling with a splash onto his back.

In its bony hand, the ghost steadied the massive sword.

The chill of the cave water welled inside Jay in a cold burn of anger. He hated the ghost. And the truth was, at that moment, he hated his father. For leaving him. For abandoning him. He felt hate. Only and eternally. He hated the living and the dead and everything in between.

Jay's body became so tense that he wasn't sure he could move. He watched, half frozen, as his father's face grimaced and the sword plunged toward his neck. He turned—just enough—as the blade splashed into the water, inches from his head.

The ghost fought to unlock the sword from the muddy ground beneath a now murky pocket of water. On his back, propped up with his elbows just above the pool's surface, he looked up at his father's shimmering face. The sword was loose again. The tip hovered two feet above his throat.

Jay had heard from both the living and the dead that your life flashes before your eyes before you die, but that wasn't what was happening at all. Instead, the lives of his friends, their very present and precarious lives, were flashing before him as he looked left and right in the blizzard of bones and metal.

He saw Danni half crawling, half swimming in the shallow pool as a ghost held out the mace, threatening to strike. He saw Brian dodging the wild swings of a scythe. He saw Pam cornered by her double in a rocky alcove, fiery tears streaming down her cheeks, an ax poised ominously above her head like a guillotine blade. Jay thought not about his own life, but about his friends, praying that somehow they would survive and could forgive him for leading them here.

He looked up at his father's face, barely visible behind the sword. And he reminded himself, over the embers of his burning rage, that this was not his father. This was just his likeness held hostage by someone else, by some*thing* else.

Jay could not, in the frenzy of the action, with a sword tip inches from his neck, recall what the ghostwriting had said. He couldn't remember if there was some bit of information he had read over the years that might allow him to overpower the purgatory ghosts. Under the circumstances, his mind could scarcely hold a thought. But as he watched his best friends splash and scramble for their lives, what Jay did know was that he didn't want his last moment to be full of venom and bitterness. He decided that, at the very least, his last moment would be just that: *his*. Were he to be trapped in this cave forever in death, he would have the memory of his last moment of life to cling to in his eternal captivity.

It was as if the lake was freezing around him, entombing him. He couldn't move his legs, but he managed to roll onto his stomach and use his arms to pull himself through the water toward the other side of the chamber. As far from his friends as possible.

The ghost trailed behind him, sword held aloft.

Jay gasped as he flung his backpack onto the rocky shore. He wriggled his upper body just out of the water. With one hand, he reached into the pack and rummaged through it until his hand felt the cool, smooth texture of glass. He removed the jar from the pack, clutched it tight in his hand, and raised his arm as high as he could.

The jar slammed against the rocks, sending glass shards and lizard guts in every direction.

"Come and get it," Jay said, his voice straining to a whisper.

The fumes from the intestines overpowered the lingering smoke of the sage. He held his breath—his last, he thought—so he wouldn't inhale the stench.

Around him the darkness dissipated and the air grew

heavy and cold as the other ghosts closed in on him from across the cave. It was working.

"Run!" Jay screamed to his friends. "Get out of the cave!"

Under drooping lids, Jay saw his shadows—one from the fiery light of each of the four ghosts—flickering against the cave walls. He rested his head against the pebbly shore and watched the ghosts stoop and kneel at the broken jar. He closed his eyes.

Across the pool, Brian shook his head as if awakening from a dream. The cave seemed dark again, like it was when they had first entered. When his eyes readjusted to the darkness, he saw Pam beside him, looking at the confused and scratched face staring back at her from the watery floor. A drop fell from a stalactite above, rippling the reflection away. Danni crouched beside them, cupping water onto her face, as if washing away the last bits of fury.

Jay opened his eyes, and the world was a shimmering blur. His breath was leaving him. He was passing into something. *So this is what it feels like,* he thought.

He heard a voice. It was faint and muffled. "Get his head up." Was that Pam? They didn't get away. They too were passing through. He had failed them. "Get his head out of the water!"

The world snapped clear and Jay's breath came back in a violent gulp. A hand clutched the collar of his shirt. He was sitting up. His eyes traced back over the hand at his chest, to an arm, a shoulder. It was Brian.

"No. Get out of here!" Jay sputtered, still delirious, as Danni ducked under his left arm.

"We need to hurry," Pam said.

The ghosts turned toward them. Shadows of swords and axes rose onto the walls around them as the ghosts drew their weapons.

Brian squinted at the ghost holding the sword. "Is that...? Wait, it's changing." His heart thumped and he had to fight to pull his gaze from the ghosts. But as he threw Jay's right arm over his shoulder, his rising anger diffused, as if running out of him into the water.

They heaved Jay off the cave floor. As they carried him toward the cave's entrance, Jay's toes dragged over the face of the pool, gliding like the ghosts giving chase behind them. Nearing the entrance, Jay could feel the chill of the ghosts on his back. The water that had soaked into the back of his shirt turned to ice. A blue glow gleamed against the cave's fangs. He braced himself.

The last thing Jay heard was a clash of violent shrieking just as he was carried under the twin stalactites.

Pam turned back and saw the ghosts contorting in agony in the cave entrance. She watched the semblance of her face cringe in torturous pain. The agonized look disappeared as the face faded back into a featureless slab, and the ghosts floated, flames cutting through the pool, back into the confines of their prison.

When Jay came to, he found himself perched on top of his

bike, which was magically riding itself through the forest. He turned his head slightly and realized that it was leaning on Pam's shoulder as she walked beside it. On the other side, Brian pushed the bike's handlebars.

"Where are your bikes?" Jay asked.

"We left them back at the cave," Brian said.

Jay hopped off the bike. His legs felt sore but they held. "I can walk it the rest of the way."

They moved as fast as the dark and their exhaustion would let them. Jay kept his head down, eyes locked on the front tire of the bike as he rolled it over the forest trail. Nobody said a word. It wasn't until they stepped out of the forest and into the open night that Danni finally spoke, breaking the silence.

"Thanks, Jay."

"For what?" he asked.

"You know, the whole sacrificing-yourself-to-save-us-from-getting-killed thing."

"Oh, that." Jay let out an exhausted laugh. "You would have done the same thing," he said. "You did. You came back for me."

Out in the open, the night air felt colder and the wind blew, chilling their wet clothes. Brian reached into his backpack—it had been soaked—and pulled out the sarinium hat. Beads of water still collected on its threads.

"Hey, Danni," Brian said, tugging the hat over his ears, "who was that?"

"Huh?"

"That guy. Your ghost."

"I don't know. Just some random face, I guess." Danni scratched her left eye.

"But—"

"That was the sword in the crystal ball," Jay said, changing the subject. "Guess it does work."

"Except for me," Pam said, looking more glum than ever.

"Not yet," Jay said.

"Not ever. I mean, let's face it, Jay. I'm supposed to be psychic, and I'm the only one whose vision in the crystal ball didn't come true. When it comes to reading tea leaves, I'm dyslexic. And every time I try to use the spirit board, all I see is *my name*! And it didn't happen just once," Pam continued. "It happened *three* times."

"No, it didn't," Brian said. He looked out at the night sky as if reading the stars.

"What?" Jay asked.

"Yeah, what?" Pam echoed.

"I can't believe I missed it," Brian said. He chuckled.

"Missed what?" Danni asked.

"We assumed Pam kept finding her name on the spirit board, but that's not what happened at all. When she asked what Pross was looking for in the library, the letters were P, M, and A. Yes, those can be unscrambled to spell 'Pam,' but they also can be unscrambled to spell 'map.' Map—the book map to the key."

"I guess," Jay said. "What about the second time?"

"'Who is looking for the glass?'" Brian said, without missing a beat. "The Association for Paranormal Matters. The APM. They're looking for the glass too. I mean, think about it."

"And the third time?" Pam said. "Jay asked me how we'd find the next clue and then—"

"We amplified the recording," Jay said. "Amp. A-M-P."

Brian shook his head, and the moonlight bounced off the silver threads of his cap. "Look, I hate to admit it, but I think we might have a bona fide psychic on our hands."

For the first time since they entered the forest, Pam smiled.

# CHAPTER TWENTY-ONE

## THREE AND A HALF PICTURES

J ay sat on his bed reclining against two stacked pillows, *The Encyclopedia of the Paranormal* open on his chest. He reread the entry about purgatory ghosts; then, as the EP suggested, he turned to the next page, to the entry on Purgatory Ghost Paralysis. He thoroughly read both the entry and the ghostwriting beside it.

With a world-weary sigh, he closed the book and pulled out his laptop. As he clicked from site to site, he found that the Internet didn't have much to add on the subject. Mortals, it seemed, didn't know much about purgatory ghosts. Maybe it was because no one had ever survived them.

The chime of Jay's video chat rang, breaking his concentration. It was Danni.

"Hey," he said, clicking the video chat to full screen.

"It was a forgery."

"What?"

**(Posing *cont.*):** believe that up to 5 percent of the world's population may be ghosts pretending to be human. Some posing ghosts are indistinguishable from humans other than the fact that their movement in the world is restricted due to being bound to a place or object (see Tethering, page 293). Certain telltale signs may indicate the presence of a posing ghost, including electrical disturbances, cold spots, and unblinking eyes. Even with potent spirit energy, posing ghosts can only maintain solid form for a limited time before they begin to fade into a vaporous apparition and eventually move on to the Other Side.

**Purgatory Ghost Paralysis:** Purgatory Ghost Paralysis (PGP) is a psychophysical condition caused by ghosts found in Pockets of Purgatory (see page 259). The condition strikes those in close proximity to the ghosts, filling them with an all-consuming rage. The anger eventually takes control of a person's thoughts and actions. A person's free will is soon eclipsed, and the body becomes a puppet of the anger. The anger cannot be escaped, quelled, or suppressed. The only way to free oneself of the paralysis is to divert one's thoughts outside oneself—to think of others, particularly those with whom bonds are strong. Only then can the mind break free from PGP, and one's thoughts and actions again become one's own.

**Pyromancy:** Pyromancy is the practice of divination by fire. As with a crystal ball, the psychic gazes into the fire until the flames or smoke begins to form images. The images may predict the future or answer a question that the psychic has posed. Rituals are often conducted to aid pyromancy, including burning laurel leaves, tossing salt into the fire, and

260

"The letter. I put it in my oven and then used a magnifying glass to compare it to the other letters."

"You sure?"

"I read up on handwriting analysis, and there are some discrepancies."

"Pross?"

"No," Danni replied. "I analyzed his signature too. He didn't write this."

"Huh."

"I'll tell you, though, whoever forged this letter was an expert."

"We shouldn't talk about it now," Jay said. "I used video chat before, and then we got the fake letter."

There was a knock at the door.

"I gotta go," he said. "If you find anything else, tell me in person tomorrow." Jay closed the video chat and snapped his laptop shut. He leaned over the side of his bed and set the computer on the floor.

"Come in," he said.

Mrs. Winnick eased open the door and walked toward Jay. "You feeling all right?" She was holding something.

"Yeah, I'm fine."

She sat down at the edge of Jay's bed. "You just seemed quiet during dinner. You didn't complain about how gross it was. Not even the organic kale."

"I thought that went without saying."

Mrs. Winnick smiled for just a moment before her look of concern returned. "You sure you're okay?"

# CHAPTER TWENTY-ONE

"I just have a lot on my mind," he said. "School stuff."

"If you say so," she said. Jay could tell she didn't believe him. "I wanted you to have something." She handed him a framed photograph: It was picture of her with Jay and his dad. They were at a climbing wall, each hanging from a harness. Jay's dad was perched triumphantly at the top of the wall. Jay was close behind, and his mom dangled beneath him, all twisted up in her harness, tilted so that she was almost upside down. Huge, teeth-baring smiles stretched across their faces.

Jay looked at his mom in the photo, dangling in hysterics, and he thought how long it had been since she had smiled like that. She hadn't always been a worrier. That had come over time; it had settled and grown insidiously like the wrinkles at the corners of her eyes. Seven years ago, she'd been willing to hang upside down from a harness twenty feet in the air and, even more amazingly, was willing to let Jay climb right alongside her.

She looked at his nightstand. "I realized you didn't have one of all three of us."

"Thanks, Mom," he said as they both looked wistfully at the picture.

She tapped him on the leg and got up from the bed.

"Hey, Mom," Jay called just before Mrs. Winnick closed the door.

"Yes?"

"I'm sorry."

"For what."

"For making you worry so much and stuff."

"It's okay."

After she closed the door, Jay put the new photograph on his nightstand right between the other two pictures of his father. He pulled out the photo of the orbs and decided to leave that on the stand as well.

Tomorrow, he and his three best friends would set out again to find the key that would unlock the Dominion Glass. The glass that could be the answer to his prayers. The glass that was so dangerous it needed to be protected from those who sought to invoke its power.

He reached down and slid the book from beneath his bed. He unbuckled the four clasps, opened the book to the newest riddle, and set it down on his nightstand next to the three and a half pictures of his father. He laid the pneumaticles on top. His racing mind quickly gave way to his exhaustion.

He fell asleep and began to dream.

YOUR QUESTIONS WILL BE ANSWERED IN:

# GHOSTS OF ROCKVILLE
## Journey to the Cliffs of Death

WHO IS FOLLOWING THE GHOST HUNTERS?

HAVE WE MET ANY OTHER APM SECRET AGENTS?

WHO IS PROSS WORKING FOR?

WILL JAY FIND HIS FATHER?

WHAT OTHER SHOCKING TWISTS AWAIT?

# BOOK TWO!

**In the groundbreaking *Ghosts of Rockville* series!**

Join Jay and his fellow ghost hunters as they battle banshees, foil phantoms, and exorcise elementals on a quest equal parts harrowing and hilarious. Featuring dozens of all new interactive MagicView™ pages, *Ghosts of Rockville: Journey to the Cliffs of Death* packs a paranormal punch full of suspense, action, and mystery, culminating in a shocking twist that will have readers begging for more.

❖ **Go to GhostsofRockville.com for more information.** ❖

**About the author:**
Justin Heimberg is a best-selling author who has sold over one million books including books in the *Would You Rather...?* and *Worst Case Scenario* series. He has also worked as a screenwriter for major movie studios and in prime-time network television.

## ❖ Acknowledgments ❖

Thanks to my family for teaching me all I ever needed to know about life and death and all the little things in between—to Dad, who showed me the value of friendship and humor; and to Mom, who taught me to believe in the best in people.

Thanks to Marisa for making every day worth living.

Thanks to Pete Fornatale for making sure I got my story straight, and for doing big-budget work at miniscule-budget rates. Thanks to Junko Miyakoshi for her patience, hard work, and collaboration—it feels like we've been through a war.

Thanks to David Gomberg, Robert Kempe, Elizabeth Herr, and everyone at Seven Footer, Lazoo, and PGW, especially David Ouimet for his support and for making me write this thing in the first place. Thanks to Bob Fuhrer for finding the magic, and to Takeshi Kubodera for making sure it wasn't lost. Thanks to Chris Schultz and Christina Askounis for your notes, thoughts, and support.

Best regards to Alex Cheung for providing the "magic" behind MagicView.

Lastly, thanks to Rockville, the real one, for its wondrous and beautiful normalcy.